Because all men
are created equal...

June O'Donal

The Fryeburg Chronicles: Book II

A Secret and a Promise

By June O'Donal

XULON PRESS

Table of Contents

Acknowledgements

I am a story teller; I am not a historian, or an artist, a cabinetmaker or a rug hooker. I am indebted to many people who have made *Book II A Secret and a Promise* possible.

My first step in writing historical fiction is to research Fryeburg and American history for the given time period. Once the historical events and facts are established, I weave my story of the Miller family to include them. Thank you to the dedicated volunteers of the Fryeburg Historical Society who staff the Research Library in North Fryeburg. Your assistance in researching the early years of Fryeburg Academy, the Oxford House and the Judah Dana House was invaluable.

I would like to thank the talented staff and volunteers at Colonial Williamsburg who assisted me with my research during my visit in August of 2011. The house tours provided inspiration. The staff at the Cabinetmaker's and Milliner's shops patiently answered my numerous questions and allowed me to photograph them at work. The tour guide at the DeWitt Wallace Decorative Arts

Museum provided me with much information about period furniture.

Everything I learned about rug hooking I learned from Janet Conner from Hiram, Maine. Visit her website www. jconnerhookedrugs.com to learn more. When I complete my rug, I will post it on face book.

Jon Marshall, a good friend and very talented artist from Denmark, Maine provided me with books and explained to me the fundamentals of making oil paints. To view some of his art work, visit www.jonallanmarshall. com.

My books have evolved into a family project! My husband Wayne and son Tim built a cider press in our basement this winter. Yes, the cider is delicious. In the past, Wayne built a model of birch bark canoes and made all the ribs and full size gunwales for a future canoe. For this book, he spent hours drawing original sketches of the cider press and Fryeburg Academy and duplicating other drawings I discovered in my research.

This computer-incompetent mother is grateful to her talented children. Thank you, Tim, for being my on-call, tech support personnel, teaching me the difference between left click and right click and finding the superscript button for my end notes. I would like to thank my daughter, Perry, for getting *The Fryeburg Chronicles* on Facebook.

About the Cover: Timothy O'Donal and Gabrielle Haire pose as Benjamin Miller and Hannah Chase, in the fields of Harnden's farm in East Fryeburg, Maine. Photography is by Perry O'Donal. Hannah's costume is designed and made by Debbie Haire. My thanks to Ralph Roth lending us Benjamin's period costume

Join us on Facebook to see photos of our cider press and birch bark canoe plus the cabinet maker's shop and dress maker's shop at Colonial Williamsburg.

We hold these truths to be self-evident,
that all men are created equal,
that they are endowed by their Creator
with certain inalienable Rights,
that are among these Life, Liberty and the Pursuit of
Happiness

The Declaration of Independence

What doth the Lord require of thee?
But to do justly,
And to love mercy
And to walk humbly with thy God.

Micah 6:8

Chronology of Historical Events

1786 – Shays' Rebellion

1787 – The Constitutional Convention

1789 – George Washington is elected as 1st President of the United States

1790 – Philadelphia becomes the nation's capital

1792 –The opening of Fryeburg Academy
The U.S. Mint is built in Philadelphia
The U.S. monetary system is installed
The Fugitive Slave Act is passed

1793 – George Washington is reelected for his 2nd term

1795 –The new Congregational Church in Fryeburg is built

1797 – John Adams is elected as the 2nd President of the United States

1799 – Ephraim Weston and family moves to Fryeburg

1800 - Washington D.C. becomes the new U.S. Capital
The Oxford House is built by James Osgood

1801 – Thomas Jefferson is elected as the 3rd President of the United States.

1802 – Daniel Webster teaches at Fryeburg Academy

1803 – The Louisiana Purchase

1804 – Lewis and Clark and the Corp of Discovery begins
their explorations
1805 – The death of Reverend William Fessenden
1806 – The dedication of the second Fryeburg Academy
building.

The Cast of Characters

There are three types of characters in this book: fictional characters, local historical characters and national historical characters.

Fictional Characters

The Miller family, Benjamin's associates in Philadelphia, Joshua Pierce and Katie Wiley are fictional characters. The character of Benjamin Miller as an adult was inspired by the real Judah Dana and the real Paul Langdon, both of Fryeburg.

Local Historical Characters

Moses Ames – one of the early settlers arriving in 1763, settling on Lot #4 of the original Seven Lots. He served on the committee to build the first meeting house in 1778 and as the first post master of Fryeburg from 1798-1808. At one time he owned a slave named Limbo, whom he sold to Col. Samuel Osgood for a yoke of oxen.

Judah Dana – is the inspiration for the adult Benjamin Miller. He was the first attorney in Oxford County arriving in Fryeburg in 1798. He served as district attorney of Oxford County 1805-1811, judge of probate 1811-1822, judge of Common Pleas 1811-1823, a delegate to the convention that framed the state constitution of Maine and briefly served as U.S. Senator of Maine. His large, colonial home built on the corner of River Street and Main Street was the inspiration for Benjamin's promise.

Reverend William Fessenden – A native of Cambridge and a graduate of Harvard College in 1768 he arrived in Fryeburg in 1774 to serve as the pastor of the Congregational Church. John Stuart Barrows described him: "He was faithful to his profession, visiting his parishioners regardless of the weather, going to the bedsides of the sick and dying, attending funerals on snowshoes. He was a man who took his duty with full consciousness of the responsibility." When viewing early marriage records in Fryeburg I noticed he officiated at nearly all of them. He also played a vital role in the founding of Fryeburg Academy serving on the first Board of Trustees and a teacher. He died on May 5, 1805.

Paul Langdon – is the inspiration for the adult Benjamin Miller. The son of Rev. Samuel Langdon, who was the President of Harvard College during the American Revolution, he graduated from Harvard and served in the Continental Army. He served as Fryeburg Academy's first preceptor from 1792- 1799. He was well known for his knowledge of classical languages. His students said of him, "More Greek and Latin in Master Langdon's forefinger than in most men's heads." He lived in a house near the first Fryeburg Academy Building near Pine Hill.

Limbo – was born a free man in Guinea, Africa and captured by slave traders while he was out feeding silk worms. Little is known about his early life or arrival to America. He was a slave of William McClellan of Gorham in the District of Maine. He spent the winter of 1762-63 watching cattle, even before the settlement of the Seven Lots. He ran away from his master and settled in Pequawket (Fryeburg). There he became the slave of Moses Ames. Tradition says that Mr. Ames treated him unkindly and Samuel Osgood compassionately bought him for a yoke of oxen. In 1790 he was sold to Samuel's son, Lt. James Osgood for five shillings. He died at the age of 90 in December of 1828 and is buried in the Village Cemetery. There is no historical evidence that he was literate or part of the Underground Railroad.

James Osgood – Son of Samuel Osgood, he built the first Oxford House in 1800 and bought Limbo for 5 shillings from his father.

Ephraim Weston – arrived in Fryeburg in 1799 with his family and purchased 46 acres from Captain Henry Young Brown, the founder of Brownfield. Today Weston's Farm and Market, a thriving business and local landmark, is still in the Weston Family.

National Historical Characters

Abigail Adams – patriot, wife of John Adams and the second First Lady of the United States

John Adams – patriot, member of the Continental Congress, the first vice-president of the United States and the Second President of the United States for one term.

Napoleon Bonaparte – a French military and political leader who rose to power during the French Revolution, he served as the Emperor of France 1804-1815 and made possible the Louisiana Purchase.

William Clark – was appointed by President Thomas Jefferson in 1804 to co-lead the Corps of Discovery to explore the newly acquired territory of the Louisiana Purchase.

Benjamin Franklin – arguably the most popular man in America, he served as patriot, printer, inventor, ambassador, and as a member of both the Continental Congress and the Constitutional Convention.

Alexander Hamilton – an ardent federalist, he served as the Secretary of the Treasury under President Washington and devised the new republic's monetary system.

Thomas Jefferson – served as Secretary of State under George Washington, vice-president to John Adams before serving two terms as the third President of the United

States. The Louisiana Purchase was acquired during his administration.

Meriwether Lewis – was appointed by President Thomas Jefferson in 1804 to co-lead the Corps of Discovery.

James Madison – played an important role at the Constitutional Convention in Philadelphia in 1787, defended the constitution in the writings of the *Federalist Papers*, served as President Jefferson's Secretary of State before being elected as the fourth President of the United States in 1808.

Daniel Shays- a Massachusetts farmer, who fought at the Battle of Lexington and the Battle of Bunker Hill, led a post-Revolution clash between New England Farmers and merchants, known today as Shays – Rebellion, which threatened to plunge the new Republic into a civil war.

George Washington – served his country as Commander-in-Chief of the Colonial forces, chairman of the first Continental Congress, and two terms as the first President of the United States from 1789-1797.

Daniel Webster – a leading American statesman and senator from Massachusetts during the period leading up to the Civil War. He served briefly as Preceptor of Fryeburg Academy in 1802.

I

The Homecoming

Six-year-old Libby Miller, peering through the second-story bedroom window, was the first to see the wagon pull up to the farm house. "Uncle Benjamin is here! Uncle Benjamin is here!" she shrieked as she ran barefoot down the front staircase, and out the front door.

Twenty-five-year-old Benjamin Miller hopped down from the wagon just in time to greet his oldest niece. "Uncle Benjamin, I have waited my whole life to meet you!"

Benjamin bent down and picked up the exuberant little girl. "And whom might you be?" he teased.

"Uncle Benjamin, I am Elizabeth Peabody Miller. But everyone calls me Libby. Are you not happy to finally meet me?"

"Heaven help us all! You are as precocious and loquacious as your mother!"

"I heard that!" laughed Grace Peabody Miller. "Benjamin, it is wonderful to have you back home after all these years. Mercy, Libby! Where are your shoes?"

"Grace, you are more beautiful than ever. Motherhood becomes you," he affectionately hugged his sister-in-law. "And whom might this be?" he smiled warmly at the shy, four- year- old girl hiding behind her mother's skirt and sucking her thumb.

"Uncle Benjamin," Libby squirmed out of his arms, "may I have the honor of presenting my little sister, Sarah Alden Miller, to you?"

Benjamin knelt by the little girl and quietly spoke, "It is my pleasure to meet you, Sarah Alden Miller."

She pulled her thumb out of her mouth. "My name is Sadie."

"Sadie, my name is Uncle Benjamin. I am your Papa's brother."

"Uncle Ethan is Papa's brother," she turned to her mother.

"Papa has two brothers," Grace explained, "Uncle Ethan and Uncle Benjamin."

Twenty- eight-year-old Micah Miller rounded the corner of the house and greeted, "Well, the Prodigal Son has finally returned home. I see you have met the family," he looked lovingly at his wife and daughters.

James Miller slowly limped down the front stairs with his wife Sarah by his side. "My son, the famous attorney from Philadelphia, has arrived," he smiled proudly.

"Benjamin," Sarah Miller opened her arms out to her middle son as her eyes brimmed with tears. Sarah deeply loved all three of her sons, but she and Benjamin shared a special bond since his twin sister Abigail died twelve years ago back in 1780. Benjamin swallowed the lump in his throat as he embraced his mother.

"I did not know the two of you knew each other," Libby stated in surprise.

"Your grandmother is Uncle Benjamin's mama, just like I am your mama. Uncle Benjamin was born and grew up on this farm just like you," Grace explained.

"Let me take a look at you," Sarah stood back and carefully inspected him. "Mercy, you look just like your Uncle Jacob."

Jacob Bradford was Sarah's older brother and Benjamin's favorite uncle. While Benjamin was studying law at Harvard College in Cambridge, he spent his summers at Uncle Jacob's farm in nearby Lexington. Micah and Ethan had reddish blond hair and blue eyes like their father; whereas Benjamin had dark brown hair and brown eyes like his mother and the rest of the Bradford clan. A late bloomer, he had left for Harvard College in the summer of 1784 at the age of seventeen as a lanky and awkward young man. Not as tall or rugged as the two brothers who had remained on the family farm by the Saco River in Fryeburg, he was almost six feet tall.

"I cannot believe that you are finally home." Although her dark hair was now streaked with gray, Sarah Miller was still an attractive and gracious woman.

"I cannot yet believe it myself. Events unfolded so quickly."

"Son, we are so proud of you," James shook his son's hand. "Welcome home."

"Mama, who is that pretty lady in the wagon?" Libby pointed.

"Where are my manners?" Benjamin gasped as he ran to the far side of the wagon and helped the attractive, slender woman down. He led her around the wagon and, still holding her hand, introduced his family. "Hannah, may I present to you my father, James Miller."

"Mr. Miller, Benjamin has told me so much about you. It is indeed an honor to finally meet you," she spoke quietly and politely.

"This is my mother, Sarah Miller."

"Mrs. Miller, you are exactly as Benjamin described you."

"This is my brother, Micah."

The young woman stared into Micah's blue eyes and smiled. Hannah had assumed Benjamin's brothers both looked like him. "And this must be the Amazing Grace with the golden petticoats. Benjamin told me how you arrived in Fryeburg from Boston during the war with gold coins sewed into the seams of your petticoats."

The family glanced at one another in bewilderment. Who was this stranger who knew so much about them? Grace thought this mysterious woman looked like a Spanish princess or a Greek goddess with her thick, black, wavy hair. Long, black eye lashes framed her gray eyes. Although plainly dressed in a simple dark gray dress, white linen bonnet and white apron, there was an air of elegance and refinement about her.

"Everyone, this is Hannah Chase, my betrothed."

There was a simultaneous gasp of surprise. Perhaps no one was more surprised than Hannah Chase herself. Sarah was the first to speak. "The Lord took one daughter and now he has given me two! Welcome to the Miller Family, Hannah." Sarah warmly embraced her future daughter-in-law. Unaccustomed to such display of maternal affection, Hannah shyly returned the embrace.

"I must tell you, Benjamin, you never mentioned in your letters that you were courting a young lady," Grace scolded good-naturedly. "Hannah, you must tell me everything!" she invited as she took her arm and headed up the stairs. In a panic, Hannah turned to a sheepishly smiling Benjamin for guidance.

Hannah's eyes widened as she entered the foyer. "Everything is exactly as Benjamin described it," she thought to herself as she studied the oak wardrobe standing at the foot of the elegant staircase. She quickly glanced at her image in the looking glass hanging over the Elizabethan oak chest, before entering the drawing room. She was immediately drawn to the contents of the two matching bookcases flanking the fireplace.

"Do you enjoy reading?" Sarah inquired.

"Yes, Ma'am, I love reading more than anything. Except for praying," she qualified her answer. Hannah, who was reverently studying the Chippendale desk in front of the fireplace, failed to notice Sarah's amused smile. "Benjamin, this must be the desk at which you sat for hours pretending to be an attorney like John Adams."

"There is no need to pretend now," Benjamin reminded her. Micah felt his brother was boasting.

After glancing at the gold and white upholstered settel and the two wing-backed chairs by the side windows, Hannah pronounced, "Truly this room is conducive to study and quiet meditation. What a beautiful view of the river," she gasped as she looked out the window. "The Lord can create anything more glorious than man can manufacture. There is no view as tranquil as this in all of Philadelphia." Hannah entered the dining room closely followed by Libby and Sadie who were enthralled with their visitor.

Admiring the portrait of Elizabeth Peabody painted by John Singleton Copley, Hannah stated in a direct and unassuming manner, "Grace, you are even more beautiful than your mother. What a magnificent dress," she admired the gold brocade dress with the pearl beaded bodice.

"I wore that dress for my wedding. It was a comfort to me for my mother died when I was thirteen. I felt a part of her was with me on my special day. Will your parents be able to travel from Philadelphia to attend the wedding? They are welcome to stay with us."

Hannah turned to Benjamin who intervened on her behalf, "No, her family will be unable to attend. She lived with her great aunt and uncle in Philadelphia and helped them run their boarding house until failing health forced them to sell the property." He quickly changed the subject. "This next room is the original portion of the house. Try to imagine six of us living in this one room with the hearth. My parents' bedroom and Abigail's room was in the space now occupied by the pantry. Up there was a sleeping loft for us boys."

"This must be the Liberty Table. Benjamin told me how you declared your independence back in July 1776 by chopping down the King's Pine on your property and building this trestle table. Truly this will be a family heirloom passed down through generations of Millers."

"Please have a seat," Sarah invited. "It is hours past the noon meal and hours still to our evening meal, yet you must be hungry and thirsty after your journey. I will reheat some vegetable soup and cornbread. I believe you gentlemen will not protest in taking a midafternoon break from farming," she smiled. "Benjamin, we have added an extra bed, wardrobe and dresser to Ethan's back bedroom, upstairs."

"Is he still afraid of the dark?" he teased.

"Oh, no. Uncle Ethan is very brave," Libby assured.

Grace turned to Hannah, "I believe you shall be most comfortable in Papa's bedroom across the hall."

"Grace, I am so sorry for your loss," interjected Benjamin. "Your father was a kind and generous man. It was his generosity that paid my tuition at Harvard and his kindness in introducing me to the partners of Templeton and Penn law firm in Philadelphia. A young and inexperienced man such as me would never have been offered a position without a personal recommendation by such an admired and successful businessman as William Peabody."

"It was merit and not nepotism which commended you, brother," Grace assured.

"William was a much-loved member of this family and my best friend. I dearly miss him," James stated solemnly.

"He often said that the last eight years of his life were by far the most meaningful. After years of captivity by the British, he was able to give his daughter in marriage and cherish the births of his three grandchildren," Sarah continued.

"I am grateful that he did not live to see the day we lost Baby William," Grace added sadly. Micah silently reached across the table and held her hand.

"Where is Ethan?" Benjamin broke the uncomfortable silence.

"Uncle Ethan is in his woodworking shop. He does not wish to be disturbed," Libby explained in her most authoritative tone.

Smiling, Sarah clarified, "Uncle Ethan does not wish to be disturbed ten times a day by his adoring nieces. I am confident that he shall not be vexed by a visit with Uncle Benjamin."

Libby leapt from the table and headed for the back door. "Elizabeth, what are the rules?" Grace asked.

"No one may be barefooted in Uncle Ethan's shop because you might step on a nail or get a splinter and it could get infected then you would have to cut off your feet and die."

"Please put your shoes on."

"I do not think that will be necessary if Papa carries me," she smiled coyly at her father.

"The acorn does not fall far from the tree," Benjamin shook his head.

Sadie began to pout as her father picked up Libby. "Sadie, may I carry you into Uncle Ethan's shop?" Benjamin offered. First she shyly looked to her mother and then to her grandmother for assurances before consenting to be carried by this stranger.

"Is this the new barn? It is huge! It is even larger than the house," Benjamin stepped back to inspect.

"It is an eight-bent frame and it took four winters to cut, a month to raise, and a year to enclose." The pride was evident in Micah's voice." My next project is to connect the house to the barn with a back addition. No more stepping outdoors before sunrise in January to milk the cows! We now have four milk cows, six horses, four oxen and two dozen sheep, a gaggle of geese..."

"And one well-behaved rooster," Grace interrupted with a laugh.

A gander flew out of the barn honking and hissing in his attempt to frighten the unfamiliar visitors.

"Quiet, Paul Revere!" Libby slapped the goose on his beak.

"Paul Revere? Are the British coming?" Benjamin laughed.

"That silly goose is the best watch dog we ever had," Micah smiled." A horse thief could not get anywhere near this barn with Paul Revere on duty."

Benjamin found Ethan carefully planing some pine boards. He looked up in surprise. "Welcome to my library," Ethan invited.

Benjamin looked around in amazement. "I see you have added many new books to your library."

"Uncle Benjamin, everyone told me how smart you are. Do you not see this is Uncle Ethan's work shop? There are no books here," Libby explained in exasperation.

"Elizabeth, do not be impertinent," Micah scolded.

Benjamin explained with a smile, "We are merely conversing in metaphors."

Ethan explained, "We are making a joke, Libby. Uncle Benjamin likes his library and books as much as I like my workshop and tools."

"I understand now. Papa's barn is his library and his livestock are his books," Libby felt very grown up participating in such a conversation.

"I have not seen such a well-organized cabinet maker's shop in all of Philadelphia," Benjamin pronounced. On the back wall Ethan had neatly hung his saws – a hand saw, a crosscut saw used for rough cuts across the grain and a frame saw with its centrally mounted blades designed for ripping planks.

Just to the right of this collection, Ethan displayed his adze – a slightly rounded hoe-shaped tool, a short-handled broad axe, a froe, three mallets of different sizes and weights, a mortising axe and an all-purpose hatchet. Four draw knives of different shapes and sizes were indispensable in removing rough spots, trimming clapboards, carving wheel spokes, shaping barrel staves and making shingles. Nearby, an assortment of gouges, files, rifflers, chisels and rasps rested at attention in their slotted shelves - all within easy reach of Ethan's sturdy work bench located by a large window affording natural light and a view of the Saco River. Ethan had painstakingly turned and carved the matching handles of each of his tools in curly maple.

Several different types of planes sat on his bench – a long, jointer plane used for smoothing edges on boards, a short smoothing plane to touch up rough spots, a jack plane with its concave blade, an adjustable plow plane to cut grooves parallel to the edge of a board and a banding plane to cut wide valleys in boards. A long cabinet maker's clamp and smaller, hand screw clamps and vises held wood firmly into place.

A large, finely-crafted curly maple tool box sat on the floor by the bench. Its opened top revealed six shallow drawers packed with braces and bits, augers, peg cutters, screw boxes, bevels, chalklines, plumb bobs and compasses.[1]

Hannah, I would like to introduce you to my talented, younger brother, the cabinet maker, Ethan Miller."

"No, I am more like a farmer who builds furniture in his spare time," he glumly explained. In the back of the shop stood three secretary desks; the first built of walnut, the second of cherry and the third of pine. Each had three lower drawers, a fold-down writing table which, when shut, concealed several small compartments, and a bookcase built along the top. The glass doors to the book case had curtains behind the glass to protect valuable books from fading in the sunlight. [2] In the corner stood a cherry armoire.

"This is Hannah Chase..."

"They are getting married!" Libby excitedly blurted.

"Do not interrupt adults when they are speaking," Micah scolded.

"Yes, Papa. Do you not think it wonderful that I now have a new uncle and a new aunt all in one marvelous day?"

"Yes, Libby, it is indeed a marvelous day," Ethan winked." It is not every day that I learn that I will have a new sister. It is a pleasure to make your acquaintance, Miss Chase."

"Perhaps, this might be a good time to unload the wagon. I am sure Benjamin and Hannah would appreciate getting settled in their rooms before the evening meal," Sarah suggested.

Benjamin delivered Hannah's one small trunk to the first floor bedroom across the hall from the dining room. "I cannot believe that such a beautiful room is all for me." The four-poster bed had a royal blue, damask canopy and bed curtains with a matching blue and white quilt. Matching bedside cabinets on opposite sides of the bed held pewter candlesticks. Grace's grandmother's 1710

William and Mary-styled highboy was placed on one side of the fireplace. An oak rocking chair which Ethan had made for Mr. Peabody's birthday was placed by the window.

"Aunt Hannah, can we help you unpack?" Libby eagerly offered.

"Perhaps you girls and your grandmother can help Hannah in here, while the men are unloading and carrying trunks up and down the stairs," Grace hopefully suggested.

"Truly, that would be lovely," Hannah agreed as she opened the lid of her trunk. "Sadie, could you please put my brush on my cabinet." Her modest trunk contained one work apron, one flannel petticoat for the winter, two brown linsey-woolsey dresses, a modest neckerchief, and a knitted shawl. What the trunk did not contain was a warm winter cloak, additional shifts, petticoats, stockings, shoes, hats or jewelry.

"Is that all there is? Are there no more trunks to open?" Libby asked in disappointment.

Sarah smiled as she remembered Grace's arrival in March of 1781 with three wagons packed with trunks containing clothing, books, linens, tableware, spices and many other luxuries. Her husband and sons struggled to unload a Chippendale tall clock, desk and armoire. Six months later a ship filled with a mansion's worth of worldly possessions docked in Falmouth to be delivered by ox-drawn wagons. What a contrast between these two young women!

"Libby, Hannah was very wise to pack only the bare necessities. It was a long and tedious journey from Philadelphia and you know Uncle Benjamin must have packed that wagon with books! I look forward to making some new dresses and a woolen cloak. Perhaps you girls would like to help."

"Aunt Hannah, can we help? Can we? Can we?" Libby clapped her hands in excitement.

"Your kindness is overwhelming. I have never owned more than one church dress and one or two work dresses. Aunt Martha always said more than one best dress was a vanity. One clean work dress and one to be washed was sufficient. I have never had my own room before. Of course all the nice bedrooms were rented. My little bed was in the kitchen by the fireplace."

"You slept in the kitchen? Did you eat in the bedroom?" Libby giggled at her own joke.

"I was always nice and warm in the winter. I would awake before daybreak, get the fire going, jump back into bed until the fire was roaring, then dress by the fire and begin breakfast. It was a very pleasant life and I met people from all over the country."

"Is that how you met my son?" Sarah asked.

"Yes, Ma'am. It was May of 1787 and he had just arrived from Massachusetts with Mr. Rufus King, a delegate at the Constitutional Convention. He was very shy and homesick, overwhelmed by the size of the city and very nervous about his first day of work at Templeton & Penn."

"Son, what in creation is this?" James pointed to the unfamiliar objects.

"I bought three Franklin stoves. They are metal-lined fireplace inserts. A hollow baffle near the rear transfers more heat from the fire to the room's air. It relies on an inverted siphon to draw the fire's hot fumes around the baffle, producing more heat and less smoke.[3]

"That is brilliant! I should have thought of that," Ethan said.

"I am sorry, but Benjamin Franklin beat you to it in 1741. We can store them in the barn for now. I am planning to put them in my own home someday. Perhaps we will install this fall and see how they work."

"Do you mean to see if they set the house on fire?" Micah questioned.

"Many of the better homes in Philadelphia have them and they are perfectly safe if they are installed correctly.

This trunk has some gifts to be opened at the evening meal tonight. These trunks are my books and papers. Father, may I move them into the drawing room, and use the desk and bookcases? In addition to my responsibilities at Fryeburg Academy, I plan to open my law office. I realize it shall take years to build up my clientele before I could support a family. I predict someday Fryeburg will be a prosperous town and I will be the first attorney in this town.

I am willing to pay rent for the use of the room," Benjamin offered.

"I will not hear of it. Does Micah pay rent for the use of the barn? Does Ethan pay rent for the use of his workshop? We are a family and this is our home," James firmly stated. "We will deliver these trunks to Benjamin's office and those trunks upstairs to his room. You may unpack them tomorrow. I am most certain Mother intends to spend this evening hearing every detail of your life over the past eight years."

"Grandmother says we are having a celebration and we will eat in the dining room this evening. This day keeps getting better and better," squealed Libby.

"Mrs. Miller, perhaps the girls and I could set the table while you and Grace are cooking in the hearth. I know children may be a distraction in the kitchen," Hannah smiled sweetly as Grace gave her a look of gratitude.

"Now girls, you may assist me with the linens and silverware. Sadie, I shall instruct you in the proper way of folding napkins. However, only I shall handle the china and glasses. Do we understand one another?" Taking each girl by the hand, she entered the dining room.

Sadie helped her sister retrieve the white linen table cloth and napkins from the mahogany sideboard. It took all of the sisters' concentration to cover the ten-foot mahogany pedestal table perfectly and fifteen minutes for them to fold the cloth napkins properly. Hannah gracefully and efficiently set the table and praised the girls for their help. "Now, I shall instruct you on the proper use and setting of the silver ware."

It was obvious to Sarah that this simply-dressed, young woman was accustomed to serving as mistress in a gracious home. Hannah Chase was an enigma; there was much Sarah wished to learn about her future daughter-in-law.

II

Philadelphia

The entire family gathered around the Liberty Table. James was ready to say grace when there was a knock on the back door. Ethan went to answer it.

"Is it true? Did Mr. Benjamin return today?" Limbo asked as he took off his black felt hat and entered the kitchen.

"Come in and see," Ethan invited. "I will set an extra plate, for we just sat down to eat."

"Mr. Benjamin, look at you all grown up!" The African slave greeted his friend and tutor.

"Limbo, my friend, look at you, you are getting old!" Benjamin laughed as he rose from the table to shake hands. Limbo, now fifty-four years old, had a head full of gray hair. "Have you continued in your studies?"

"Oh, yes. Mr. Peabody and I started a book club. I would read one chapter a week from one of his fancy books and then we would discuss it. He had the best stories to tell about his travels. He taught me how to find the countries on his globe. It was a sad day when he passed away."

"Indeed, it was a sad day for all of us. Come join us, Limbo. We are celebrating Benjamin's return and future marriage to Hannah," James invited.

"Limbo, this is Hannah Chase," Benjamin introduced.

"Limbo, Benjamin has told me so much about you. I feel like I know you. It is wonderful to finally meet you," Hannah smiled warmly.

"It is very nice to meet you as well," he replied shyly.

"I am pleased to hear that you enjoy your new home," Benjamin smiled. In October 1790 Samuel Osgood sold Limbo for 5 shillings to his son, Lt. James Osgood. [1]

When Limbo's plate and silverware were placed on the table James instructed, "Let us pray. Our God, our King and Creator, we give Thee thanks for reuniting my family. We thank Thee for safely bringing Hannah to us, and for returning our son safely to us. We thank Thee for the strength and comfort Thou hast provided us during the past difficult months. We thank Thee for your continuing provisions and love. Amen."

"Hannah, tell us, how did you and Benjamin meet?" Grace asked eagerly.

"Benjamin arrived at my great uncle's boarding house and asked directions to the nearest bookstore," she replied innocently as the family chuckled. "Philadelphia has thirty bookstores and we visited every one that summer." [2]

"It is a bibliophile's paradise," Benjamin agreed. "Philadelphia is the center of the book trade, second only to London.[3] What an opportunity for a new attorney to arrive just as the 55 delegates from twelve states met for the Constitutional Convention."

"I thought there were thirteen states," Libby interrupted.

"You are correct but Rhode Island refused to send any delegates. Of course at the time it was not called the Constitutional Convention. The delegates were there to revise the Articles of Confederation. The work they did daily from May to September at the Pennsylvania State House was top secret.

There was a strong, widespread opposition to a constitution. Some felt that sovereign and independent states fought together for six years and won the war. Why fight a war and win independence only to be taxed by a powerful Congress instead of a powerful British Parliament?"

"Those are my very sentiments," Micah solemnly stated. "I see no need for a strong federal government. If you give them a little power, they will continually interfere with the states' rights and exert more influence and raise more taxes."

James nodded, "I fear that you are correct."

"Yes, but the Articles of Confederation did not have the power to collect taxes, to defend the country or to pay the public debt. They could not encourage trade and commerce.

The Constitution may not have been ratified if Shays' Rebellion in '86 had not frightened so many people. It threatened to plunge the 'disunited states' into a civil war. New England was on the verge of collapse,"[4] Benjamin explained.

"Daniel Shays was a real war hero," Micah disagreed. "He served in both the Battle of Lexington and the Battle of Bunker Hill. He and many other farmers were veterans who returned home after the war without a single month's pay – just worthless government certificates. Then the government heavily taxed their farmlands. When they were unable to pay, their furniture, grain and livestock was sold off for much less than their value. How is that fair? [5]

The farmers in western Massachusetts called special meetings to protest conditions. They closed the court houses by force and liberated the imprisoned debtors from jail.[6] They tried to work within the framework of government without success. Those poor farmers felt the only redress they had lay in open rebellion.[7]

How is Daniel Shays any different from Samuel Adams when they threw the tea in Boston Harbor?" Micah challenged.

"Apparently Samuel Adams believes they are very different. He said, 'Rebellion against a king may be pardoned, or lightly punished, but the man who dares to rebel against the laws of a republic ought to suffer death,'" Benjamin quoted.[8]

Raising his voice Micah countered, "Well Thomas Jefferson disagreed. He said, 'A little rebellion now and then is a good thing. It is a medicine necessary for the sound health of government. God forbid that we should ever be twenty years without such a rebellion'."[9]

"Papa, are you and Uncle Benjamin having a fight?" Libby asked.

"No, Libby, your father and uncle are having a heated political debate," Ethan explained. "It is what Americans do."

"Brother, I see marriage has served you well," Benjamin smiled.

"How do you mean?"

"Before you were married, you never expressed your opinions. You kept your thoughts to yourself. I look forward to future political discussions."

"Well I will end this discussion with the note that Daniel Shays was pardoned in 1788."[10]

"Getting back to the subject at hand," Grace interrupted, "please tell me more about how the two of you got to know one another – when you were not buying books."

"Mr. Chase hired me to tutor Hannah three evenings per week. May my Fryeburg Academy students be half as intelligent and motivated," he smiled proudly across the table.

"Benjamin was such a great teacher; his excitement for learning was truly contagious. The first night we met, I was illiterate when we visited a bookstore. One year later, I was reading his books!"

"Mama taught me to read and I have not yet begun school. Did your parents not teach you how to read?" Libby asked innocently.

"Elizabeth, children are to be seen and not heard," Micah admonished. "Do not interrupt adults when they are speaking."

"Libby, I was just a little girl when my father left to fight in the war. I remembered how hard I cried when he told me he was going to help General Washington."

"Your father personally knew George Washington?" Ethan asked.

"Yes he did. We lived but ten miles from Mount Vernon."

"Did he die in battle?" Grace inquired.

"No, he died of small pox at Valley Forge. After that my family broke up – my mother and siblings and I went in separate ways."

"Mercy!" Sarah quietly exclaimed.

"It was not my mother's choice. I went to live with Mr. and Mrs. Chase, my great aunt and uncle. They offered me a loving family, a beautiful home, plenty to eat and an opportunity to go to church. All they asked in return was some help in running the boarding house. They taught me about God's love and how to run a household, but not how to read."

"I think that was terrible!" Libby pronounced.

"Libby, there are many children who had a life like mine. You must always be thankful for your family, your home and everything you have."

Benjamin continued the story. "She was a brilliant student and an avid reader. Dear Mrs. Chase was always introducing me to proper, eligible young ladies. I preferred spending my evenings at home discussing Algernon Sidney's *Discourses Concerning Government* with my favorite student. I was terrified the first time I had to speak in a courtroom. The night before, Hannah listened to me rehearse my opening arguments. After that, I depended upon her insight and wisdom."

Sarah smiled at the couple with approval.

"Benjamin, do tell us about Philadelphia. My father spent a great deal of time there on business, and I never had the opportunity to visit," Grace said.

"Getting back to the first summer I was there. You can imagine how exciting it would be for someone who grew up in Fryeburg to see these incredible men walking to and from the state house every day."

"Did you see President Washington?" James asked in awe.

"He was not President yet. He was only General Washington then. Yes, I saw him on several occasions – at a distance. One evening, I sat and dined at a table in a tavern next to James Madison's table. The grandest sight was to see old Benjamin Franklin being carried on a sedan chair he brought back from Paris. It had glass windows on both sides. Prisoners from the Walnut Street Jail would carry the ten foot poles holding the sedan chair and its distinguished passenger. A carriage ride over the cobblestones was much too painful for his gout.[11]

"Did you see John Adams?" Sarah inquired of her best friend's husband who now served as Vice President under President Washington.

"No, he and Mrs. Adams were in London at the time."[12]

"What about Thomas Jefferson?" Micah asked.

"He is Secretary of State, now. Back in '87 he was in Paris serving as the American minister to France.[13] However, I digress. Getting back to Philadelphia…

It is the largest and wealthiest city in America. Although it is more than 100 miles from open sea it is America's busiest port with wharves stretching two miles along the Delaware River.[14] There is a social library where members pay an entrance fee and annual dues, so they may read the group's books.[15] Someday Fryeburg must establish a social library.

Unlike Fryeburg with one Congregational Church, Philadelphia has a heterogeneous culture with a wide variety of religious creeds. There are at least three Quaker meeting houses, two Presbyterian churches, one Lutheran chapel, a Dutch Calvinist church, a Roman Catholic chapel and one Anabaptist meeting house."[16]

James was uncertain how he felt about such diversity of creeds. On one hand Philadelphia had the potential to become a center for heresy. On the other hand, freedom of worship was an important tenet of American citizens' rights. Unlike England and other European countries, where wars erupted between Catholics and Protestants or minority sects like Quakers and Puritans were persecuted, America was an example where diverse churches could peacefully coexist. Christians of all backgrounds could worship unmolested by the government.

"I believe that this tolerant atmosphere in religion encouraged the interchange of books and ideas on many other subjects as well.[17] In addition to the churches and bookstores Philadelphia has some great public buildings like the State House and Carpenter Hall. The Quakers donated money to construct a new hospital, a new poorhouse and the new prison on Walnut Street.[18]

I was thrilled when Congress moved the Capital from New York City to Philadelphia last year. Do you know that they began construction on the new U.S. mint just before we left? Philadelphia is a perfect city to be the Capital."

"Then why is the government wasting our tax dollars by building a new Capital on the Potomac?" Micah demanded.

"The northern states wanted the Capital to be in a prominent city like Philadelphia, because most of these cities were in the north. The South preferred to have the Capital closer to their agricultural and slave holding interests. James Madison believed that the Capital needed to be separate from any state.

President Washington selected the land around the Potomac River which served as the boundary between Virginia and Maryland."[19]

"Both of these states are slave states," James observed.

"This location was agreed upon by Thomas Jefferson, James Madison and Alexander Hamilton," Benjamin continued.

"I can understand why Jefferson and Madison would approve for they are both Virginians. Why would Hamilton, a northerner from New York, agree to such a thing?" Grace questioned.

"Hamilton is a very shrewd politician," Benjamin observed. "He wanted the federal government to take on the debts accrued by the states during the war. By 1790 most of the southern states repaid their overseas debt. Therefore he proposed that the South assume a share of the northern debt in return for a southern location for the federal capital."[20]

"Benjamin you are omitting another reason," Hannah softly interjected. "In 1780 the state of Pennsylvania passed the Act for the Gradual Abolition of Slavery. It did not free any one. However, the future children born to Pennsylvanian slaves would be free after serving as indentured servants until the age of twenty-eight for the mother's master. It also prohibited the importation of slaves. This created a dilemma for slaveholders such as George Washington. Because anyone residing in Pennsylvania for six continuous months would be considered a resident this act would apply to his slaves. President Washington always insists that he is a Virginia resident who merely works in Philadelphia and he is always careful not to exceed the six-month limit."[21]

"That is very interesting, Hannah. I had no idea," James complimented.

"What I would like to know, if Philadelphia is such a wonderful place, why did you return to Fryeburg?" Micah asked suspiciously.

"What I really want to know," Ethan asked mischievously, "if you were making a fortune defending Tories why would you want to teach at Fryeburg Academy for fifty-two pounds sterling a year?"[22]

"Ethan, you must understand that not everyone in this country wanted the Revolution. Some believe that a third was Patriots, one third was Tories and one third remained neutral. Clearly less than one half of the population was Patriots.

Many Tories lost everything – jobs, estates, savings and sometimes their lives. Thousands fled to England or to Canada. However, many remained here in America.[23] I am not talking about traitors who took up arms against their countrymen or spies. I am talking about people who disagreed with the Patriots' call for revolution. This is America. Is it illegal to hold a differing political opinion from those currently in power?

In Pennsylvania there is a sizable Quaker population. Some were inclined to side with the king believing that 'the setting up and putting down of kings and governments is God's peculiar prerogative, for causes best known to himself.'[24] Some agreed with the Patriots in theory. However, pacifism prevented both groups from taking up arms. Some tried to remain neutral. Unfortunately many

Patriots felt the Quaker principle against war was also a principle against revolution.[25]

Quakers were not being punished for their political beliefs but for their religious beliefs. My job was to file claims for lost property for these innocent citizens."

"An honorable endeavor," James stated proudly. "I did not volunteer to fight in the war and I would not want my farm confiscated."

"Are you a Quaker, Mr. Miller?" Hannah asked.

"I lost my father as a very young child. Life was a struggle for my mother. I did not want my wife to struggle running the farm and raising the family alone if I left for war or never returned. I had many discussions with Reverend Fessenden, Dr. Emery and Mr. Frye. They felt it would be unwise to leave a town filled with women, children and the elderly totally defenseless in the wilderness. Some men were designated to remain here ready to protect and defend the town if the situation required. No, I am not a Quaker. I would fight to protect my family and property. Are you a Quaker?"

Sarah gave her husband a disapproving glance.

"Sir, I had no religious training until I arrived in Philadelphia. Out of respect for my elders, Benjamin and I attended the Quaker meetings."

"Benjamin?" Sarah looked to her son for an explanation.

"Mother, the Chases with whom I lived for five years, who treated me like family, are Quakers. Mr. Penn and Mr. Temple my employers are Quakers as well as many of our clients."

"We are Christians, Mrs. Miller. We have no objections to the Congregational Church."

"My question is," Micah persisted, "why would you leave your position in Philadelphia to teach a room full of farm boys in Fryeburg? You could not wait to leave town nine years ago."

Benjamin had not anticipated this question. He had to think quickly in order to avoid suspicion for the real reason. "Father, why did you leave your position as pastor of a Congregational Church in Cambridge and become a farmer in Fryeburg?"

"I guess I wanted the challenge of starting a farm in the wilderness. I know long after I am gone, this farm will remain for my descendants."

"Exactly," Benjamin nodded. "I am not teaching a room full of farm boys. I am establishing a new academy. Long after I am forgotten, Fryeburg Academy will still be here. I will be educating a generation of future leaders in this town, this state and in this new nation."

"Mr. Benjamin, I do not care why you are here. I am just happy to have you home," Limbo grinned.

"Amen to that!" Sarah concurred.

"I believe now would be an appropriate time to open some gifts," Benjamin changed the subject. "The ladies may wish to open this trunk," he winked at Libby. The women gasped as Libby opened up the trunk tightly packed with cotton fabric ranging in color from white to soft gray, dark green, indigo and black.

"I must tell you, this is simply beautiful," Grace complimented.

"These printed fabrics are imported from England and the latest fashion. These are block printed and those are copper plate printed," Benjamin explained.[26]

"Benjamin, I always spin and weave our own fabric," Sarah protested.

"Mother, the war is over. The United States trades with England all the time now. Spinning and weaving is old fashioned." James' disapproving glance stopped him. "What I meant to say was your time may be better spent making a warm woolen cloak and other winter items for Hannah. We will need sheets and blankets and curtains after we marry and move into a home of our own. You already have much spinning and weaving to do. Sewing outfits with some of this fabric will save you time."

"Mama, may I have a new dress?" Libby asked excitedly.

"After the harvest I shall make you and Sadie new dresses for Sundays. Next year when you turn seven and begin school, you will have a nice dress to wear. Our first priority is to make some outfits for Aunt Hannah; she certainly needs some." Grace, who always spoke her mind, did not intend to be rude.

Sarah intervened, "Benjamin, this is very lovely. All of us will be busy this winter and we shall all be gaily attired this spring."

"Libby, please hand this to your Papa," Benjamin directed.

Micah unwrapped a remnant of unbleached muslin and found a book. "It is *The Farmers' Almanac*," Benjamin smiled warmly.

Micah was tempted to respond, "I have become a successful farmer without one of your fancy, Philadelphia books." However, Benjamin appeared to be eager for Micah to like his gift. "That was very thoughtful of you.

I am sure Father and I will enjoy reading it this winter," he politely responded.

"Ethan, I also found a book I thought you might enjoy," he handed the gift to his younger brother.

"I cannot believe it! You bought me a copy of *The Philadelphia Price Book*! Every cabinet maker in America wants one of these. Now I know what to charge for a piece of furniture based on description and kind of wood.[27] Thank you!" Ethan eagerly thumbed through the pages.

"I hope the book tells you to give family discounts to your brother. I plan to have you build us some furniture after the wedding," Benjamin smiled. "Limbo, I have a book for you as well," he handed his friend a package.

The African frowned, "What kind of book is this? All the pages are blank."

"It is a journal. You write in it," Hannah explained sweetly.

"What shall I write?"

"It could be a prayer journal," Sarah suggested.

"It could be a weather journal," Micah added.

"You could draw pictures in it," Sadie said shyly.

"You could write a story about a beautiful princess who has to fight a dragon who stole her new shoes," Libby animatedly explained.

"Perhaps you could use the pages to write letters," Grace contributed.

"You could give it to me," Ethan joked. "It would be perfect to sketch furniture designs."

"Uncle Benjamin, what are those funny things in the bottom of the trunk," Libby interrupted.

"That is for your grandfather."

"I have never seen anything like these," James was baffled. "What are they?"

"They are called venetian blinds and you install them in your windows. You can raise them or lower them, open or close them to keep the sun out."

"Is this a new Philadelphia invention like lightning rods and Franklin stoves?" James asked.

"No, venetian blinds are quite old, in fact. But they are wonderful in keeping a room cooler or preventing the sun from fading your furniture. It also prevents people from peeking in your windows at night," Hannah explained. "Venetian blinds –"

"Venetian blinds are from Venus!" Libby interrupted.

The room filled with laughter as Libby's lower lip began to quiver.

"How many times have we told you not to interrupt when adults are speaking?" Grace admonished.

"Venetian blinds are from a city in Italy called Venice," Benjamin explained.

"Then why are they not called venison blinds?" Libby contradicted.

"Marco Polo brought the blinds to Venice from China in the late 1200's,"[28] explained Grace. The daughter of a successful and wealthy Boston merchant, she knew much about imported items.

"Then we shall call them Chinese blinds," Libby stated emphatically.

Sarah thought all the gifts were delightful. However the greatest gift of all was to have her family reunited.

III

A Secret

Benjamin and Hannah slowly walked down the lane heading toward the main street in Fryeburg Village. Finally, Hannah broke the silence. "Benjamin, why did you introduce me to your family as your betrothed?"

Benjamin blushed and swallowed hard before speaking. "The night before Mr. Chase had his stroke I asked him for your hand in marriage."

"Benjamin, did you truly?"

"Everything happened so quickly. First I received the letter from Reverend Fessenden offering me the position as preceptor of Fryeburg Academy. I knew I could not leave Philadelphia without you by my side. Therefore I asked Mr. Chase for your hand in marriage and he gave me his blessing. The next morning he had the stroke rendering him speechless. That night his son arrived talking about selling the house and all the property. I was afraid of what might become of you.

When I had the opportunity to ask, I lacked the courage. When I had the courage, I lacked the opportunity.

Perhaps at this moment I may possess both. Hannah, will you do me the honor of –"

"Uncle Benjamin! I have been searching for you. I am so happy to finally find you!" Libby squealed as she ran barefoot to them.

"What is it, Libby?" Benjamin failed to conceal his frustration.

Her lower lip began to quiver, "Sadie is taking a nap and Mama told me to run outside and play so she could have a minute's peace."

"Come here," Benjamin offered as the three of them sat in the shade of the maple tree. "Did you hear the story of how my sister, your Aunt Abigail died?" Libby nodded. "Well your grandmother needed a minute's peace for weeks – for months. I understand how you feel. It was a very hard time for all of us. Your mama lost her father and her baby within a few months. She needs some time to feel better. Your grandmother felt better after a while."

"What made Grandma feel better?"

"Your mother arrived on our doorstep."

Libby giggled. "I heard that story a thousand times! Papa says he never saw such a beautiful girl in his life. Did you think my mother was beautiful?"

"No, I thought she was annoying and I wanted her to return to Boston," he answered truthfully.

Libby laughed. "Please tell me the story. Papa Peabody always told the best stories. He and I would sit in the drawing room and he would tell me about all the cities he visited in his ship called the *Sweet Elizabeth*. Then he would show me on the globe all the places he visited. Have you ever seen a seagull? I want to see a seagull someday and travel on a ship. Do you tell good stories, Uncle Benjamin? Please tell me about the day my mother arrived at Riverview Farm."

"Not today. But tomorrow, I promise. Hannah and I are going to take a walk to see Fryeburg Academy."

"Oh, good! May I come too?"

"Yes you may, if you first return and put your shoes on," Hannah invited, much to Benjamin's dismay.

"I cannot. I threw them in the sheep pen."

"Elizabeth, why would you do such a thing?" Hannah asked in a maternal tone of voice.

"They hurt my toes and give me blisters."

"Your Papa made us boys' moccasins when we were growing up. I am sure if you told him your shoes were too small, he would make you a pair."

"I do not want ugly, stupid moccasins! I want to wear pretty shoes like Mama's!"

"Of course you do," Benjamin laughed out loud. "You are a Peabody."

"Why does everyone say that? Papa Peabody always said, 'James, little Sadie may be a Miller, but Libby is a Peabody through and through'."

"Mr. Peabody was a wise man," Benjamin smiled and nodded.

"I think what your grandfather meant was Sadie is quiet and reserved like your Papa. You are charming and extroverted like your Mama," Hannah sweetly explained.

"What does extroverted mean?"

"It means you talk incessantly."

"It does not, Benjamin. Libby, it means you are very friendly. That is an admirable trait to have," Hannah contradicted. "Perhaps if we explain the situation to your mother, she may give us a pair of old shoes. We can cut them up and remake smaller shoes from the leather. Every afternoon after we clean up from the midday meal we shall sit under this tree and work on the shoes. This way your Mama will have her minute of peace and we shall have our own special time together just the two of us."

"That is more than I ever dared to hope for!" Libby jumped up. "Now let us take a walk and inspect Fryeburg Academy," she grabbed her uncle's hand. "Do you know Papa gave them some of the trees to build it? Did you know that Papa, Uncle Ethan and some other men cut the timbers and put up the frame? Did you know Grandpa Miller boasts about you all the time? 'My son, the attorney in Philadelphia'... 'My son is going to be the preceptor of the new academy'... Grandma says boasting is a sin. Is that true? If it is, I am a very big sinner," she sadly shook her head. "Do you see that butterfly on the bush? I wonder what kind it is. Uncle Ethan would know. Uncle Ethan knows just about everything. Is that boasting?"

Benjamin stopped listening as he stared at the modest thirty-foot-square wooden structure at the bottom of Brown's Hill. Facing Main Street on the west, the front had two windows and a single door to the right. The south side had three large windows designed to let in natural light.[1]

"It is not the outside appearance that makes a great school; it is the learning which happens on the inside," Benjamin told himself. Libby led the way as she ran up the steps and through the door.

"Libby, where are your shoes? Does your mother know you are here all by yourself?" Reverend William Fessenden asked with concern.

"My shoes are too tight so I threw them in the sheep pen. Aunt Hannah and I are going to make me new shoes under the maple tree. I am not alone. I came with Uncle Benjamin…"

"Benjamin!" the good pastor greeted as Benjamin and Hannah entered. "Did you have a good journey?" the two men warmly shook hands.

"Hannah, may I present to you Reverend Fessenden, my pastor, my mentor and one of the founding trustees of the academy."

"They are getting married!" Libby blurted. "Is that not the most exciting thing in the world?"

"That certainly is," he smiled. "The two of you must come for a visit and get caught up on events during the past nine years. We have so much to discuss. Did you bring home any new books? You were the trustees' first choice for the position. Although many doubted that you would accept our humble offer. I am most pleased and grateful that you have. This academy has been a dream of mine for years.

Hannah, I am delighted to meet you. We will get together soon. The trustees decided to begin school after the harvest. Too many of our students would be needed at home and I fear if we started in September, we would have a high rate of absenteeism. That is no way to start a new school year at a new academy."

Benjamin had to agree with the reverend's logic, although he was disappointed not to begin right away. He looked around the large room with a fieldstone fireplace along the North wall. In two months' time, fifty scholars would fill the room.[2]

"It looks empty," Libby complained.

"It will not be empty for long. Tomorrow I will fill these shelves with books and Ethan will help me put up the large, slate writing board. But now we must return home before your mother misses you and begins to worry."

"I cannot wait until I tell her about my new shoes!" she ran out the door and headed home.

Benjamin once again worked up his courage as they slowly strolled back to the farm.

"Hannah, you know I have developed the most sincere and deep affections for you. If I may be so bold as to declare those affections are reciprocated." This was not going well. He should have made notes and practiced his speech as if he was making closing arguments in a court room.

"Dear, sweet Benjamin, no one would ever question our affections for one another. Our affections are not the issue. A man like you simply cannot marry a woman like me," she said sadly.

"But, Hannah…"

"Welcome home, Benjamin!" Lt. Osgood pulled up the wagon. "Hop in. I am on my way to Riverview Farm. Limbo told us you were getting married. Welcome to Fryeburg, Miss Chase."

Benjamin sighed as he helped Hannah into the wagon. Why did life have to be so difficult?

Benjamin hardly touched his food that evening while Libby chattered about her new shoes. Grace thought that was an excellent idea and Ethan was certain he had some leather- working tools in his shop.

"What is wrong, Benjamin?" his mother asked. "You have not said a word."

"I am fine, Mother. I just have a lot on my mind. I think a walk after supper would do me good. Hannah, let me show you the fields, the maple trees and the Saco River," he invited.

Finally, when they were safely out of earshot, Benjamin took Hannah's hand and asked, "What did you mean that a man like me cannot marry a woman like you?"

"Do not be coy, Benjamin. Do you want me to say it aloud? Fine! A white man cannot marry a slave. It is illegal."

"Marriage is a holy covenant between a man and a woman before God. I think God would disagree with your statement. 'For in Christ there is no male or female, Greek or Jew, slave or free.'

"What would your family think?"

"They will never know."

"If they did, they would not accept me."

"If they did, I believe they would love you. That is why I returned to Fryeburg, so we could have a life together. Hannah, tell me what is wrong? Why are you upset?"

"Why am I upset? You humiliated me! You bought me in front of witnesses and packed me in the wagon like a trunk of your second-hand books! Now you think I should marry you!"

He slowly slumped to the ground, leaned his back on a tree and silently closed his eyes. He had to think! He had to think how this situation must have appeared to her. He had assumed she knew what he had been thinking. How could everything go so wrong?

"Hannah," he said softly as he opened his eyes. "Please sit by me," he patted the grass. "There has been a terrible misunderstanding and I fear it is my fault." She silently sat down. "I asked Mr. Chase for your hand in marriage and he agreed that he would give you your freedom. The only reason they bought you was to ensure you had a safe and healthy childhood. You know they loved you as a granddaughter. They believed they were protecting you.

Then everything went wrong. He had the stroke the next day. His son arrived, planning to sell the house and all the property. Hannah, I had no witnesses to our agreement. Nothing was put into writing.

I went to Mr. Penn and Mr. Temple for legal advice. I went to the elders at the meeting house for spiritual counsel. They all advised me to legally purchase you from Mr. and Mrs. Chase, in writing, in front of witnesses and leave for Fryeburg immediately. In this way, no one could accuse you of being a runaway slave. No one up here would know your past. We would have a new life together. I had to redeem you before I could marry you. It was the only way. I am sorry, for I assumed you realized that.

Marry me, Hannah. Make me the happiest man in the world and marry me."

"I cannot."

"Hannah, you must let go of your past. I do not see a slave before me. I see my bride."

"I cannot."

"You would choose to remain a slave instead of being my wife, the mistress of her own household, the mother of our children – free children?"

"There is a third option. You could grant me my freedom."

Benjamin had not thought of that. "I am afraid that I am a much better attorney than I am a suitor. We have not had a proper courtship. May I court you, Hannah Chase? Shall we spend the next six months getting to know one another better? I am afraid that during the past five years I have done all the talking about my childhood, my family, my education, and my court cases. I never knew your father died at Valley Forge. Please give me the opportunity to get to know you. Then after six months if you choose your freedom over marriage, then I will grant you your freedom. You have my word."

"Will you put that in writing? Will you legally change my name to Hannah Chase?"

"Hannah Chase is not your given name?"

"It is the name Mr. and Mrs. Chase ascribed to me. My slave name is Royal Randolph. My father named me Royal because when I was born, he thought I looked like a princess. Of course my last name is Randolph because that is the name of my father and master."

Benjamin looked at her incredulously. "Your father was a member of the Randolph family from Virginia? What was his name?"

Hannah shook her head, "I do not know. I was only six-years old when he died. The white people called him Mister and the slaves called him Master." She smiled, "There are more Randolphs in Virginia than Osgoods in Fryeburg." Benjamin laughed.

Hannah grew serious. "My father was the only one who ever loved me."

"Surely your mother loved you."

"My mother despised me!" she hissed.

"That cannot be true."

"When I was three years old, she tried to drown me in the James River!"

Benjamin gasped in shock as Hannah continued. "My mother was a filthy, vile creature and I never want to be anything like her!" her voice trembled with emotion. Then calming down she continued, "Mrs. Chase told me I must forgive her. Now that I am older I must try to understand her situation and be compassionate."

"I do not understand. What was her situation?" he asked naively.

"Although my mother was very light-skinned, she had an African husband and several black children."

"Your mother committed adultery?"

"No. My father committed adultery. Although I do not believe that polite society would use that term. My father was the master; my mother was the slave. She had no choice, she was violated."

The true inhumanity of slavery was becoming evident to Benjamin for the first time as Hannah continued with her history. "My very existence was a constant reminder of that union. My black siblings hated me for being "white"; my white siblings hated me for being "black". Of course Mrs. Randolph hated me for the same reasons my mother's husband did. My father was the only person who ever showed any kindness to me."

"Why did your mother try to kill you?"

"When I was three years old, my father sold my mother's husband. I did not know or understand that at the time. I guess she was trying to take revenge against him. My father took away someone she loved so she would take away someone he loved."

"I am so sorry, Hannah. I had no idea."

"She did me a favor. My father realized that I would never be safe living with them, so he brought me up to his big house where I spent every day. I would go home at night to sleep with Emma the cook. She taught me how to polish the silver, to set the table, to dust the furniture. My father spent time with me every day that he was home. He made me feel that I was really his little princess. I missed him terribly when he left. He gave strict instructions that my situation was not to change in his absence. When he died, the first thing Mrs. Randolph did was to sell me.

Although Mr. and Mrs. Chase believe that slavery is an abomination, they felt they were serving the Lord by buying innocent young slave girls to protect them from abuse. They already had one slave named Lilly. They told me that I was to be Lilly's apprentice. When she married and had her own family, I was appointed housekeeper and hostess.

I cried when they changed my name from Royal to Hannah."

"Why would they do that?"

"They said that the name Royal was a vanity for it implied I was better than others. Hannah was a godly name meaning favor or grace. I am thankful now that they did change it.

Mrs. Chase also said that my beauty would be my downfall. Men would like me for the wrong reasons. Is that why you wish to marry me?"

As an attorney, he recognized a loaded question when he heard one. "I am the first to admit that you are indeed a beautiful woman. Remember Proverbs 31:30 'Charm can be deceitful, and beauty fades, but a woman who reveres the Lord shall be greatly praised.' Your inward beauty far outshines your outward beauty." He was relieved when Hannah appeared to be pleased with his praise.

"Hannah, how can I live my life without you? How could I have won all of my court cases, if I did not have you to recite my arguments? With whom would I discuss philosophy, theology and politics? How can I face a classroom of scholars without you to discuss my lessons? Without you, I would be alone."

"My dear, sweet Benjamin, you have given me much to ponder. You may court me," she smiled. "You may court me."

IV

The Harvest

Benjamin was so involved in his lesson plans, he did not hear Hannah enter the classroom and walk up to his desk.

"Your family needs you," she spoke quietly.

Startled, he quickly put down his quill. "What happened? What is wrong?"

"It is harvest time and there is more work to be done than they can manage. Your father is no longer a young man and Grace has her hands full with the girls."

"They managed the past eight harvests without me. I trust they can manage one more."

"Arrogance does not become you, Benjamin Miller," she replied quietly.

"How is a man working at his job arrogant?" he demanded angrily. "I need this job for it will be years before my law practice expands to the point where I can support a family. School will be starting in six weeks and I must be prepared."

"It is only fair, Benjamin, as we are living in their home, eating their food, being warmed by their hearths that we help in the harvest. You have evenings to study. I truly understand that you are anxious to please Reverend Fessenden and the other trustees. It is your joy of learning that will make you a great teacher – not trying to impress your elders with your knowledge. Perhaps you are too eager to impress your father and brothers with your station in life. I think they would be more impressed if you left your scholarly sanctuary to help on the farm."

He never remembered his mother speaking to his father in such a manner. "Those are difficult words to hear," he warned.

"Perhaps they are difficult to hear for you know they are true," she simply stated.

His anger melted into shame. "I fear that you do speak the truth."

"They were difficult words to say," she admitted. "There is honor and dignity in working with your hands as well as with your head."

"How could I ever manage without you?" he flattered.

"I fear you would not manage very well."

He laughed at her intense sincerity. "This is why you must marry me, and soon!" he boldly took her into his arms and kissed her on the mouth.

"A gentleman does not take liberties with a lady," she smiled coyly.

He hung his head in mocked dejection. "I have been rightfully rebuked," he shook his head, "yet I remain unrepentant!" He kissed her again.

"I fear, sir, that if we tarry we shall both have much to repent."

"This is why we must marry. We should celebrate our passions and not fear them."

"Is celebrating your passions the only reason you wish to marry?" she challenged.

"I hope I win all my arguments in the courtroom for I fear I will win none in my home," he laughed.

She smiled brightly, wisely saying nothing as she led him out of the classroom and into the September air.

"I am at your service, Sir." Benjamin offered as he entered the barn dressed in his work clothes.

His father smiled in relief. "Perhaps you could pick the pumpkins and load the wagon with me. This will free up Ethan who needs to finish building the cider press. This is the best year our orchard has had. The ladies are out picking apples and the girls are picking up the drops and putting them into baskets. We can perhaps begin making cider tomorrow."

Benjamin had to admit that the sunshine and fresh air was invigorating. However, it was disheartening to see how his father had aged during the past eight years. Simply getting in and out of the wagon was painful, for his old injury had not healed properly. Benjamin picked all the pumpkins while his father drove the wagon.

"Forgive me, Father for not helping sooner."

"I know you are anxious to do your job well. I told your brothers as soon as you felt prepared for class, you would be out here helping us." Benjamin did not want to admit that it was Hannah who cajoled him to leave his books. "This will give us a chance to talk about your classes."

"Sir, I must confess that I am overwhelmed. There is Greek and Latin to teach as well as the Classics to read. However, there is also much to learn about our own new nation. Alexander Hamilton has just introduced a new monetary system…"

"I have not heard about that. That is a lesson unto itself."

"Then there is the new Constitution and the Bill of Rights and the Federalist Papers."

"I think our young citizens should be well versed in that. Son, teach what you know. Your students will respect you for it."

"Yes, Sir. Father, have you ever wondered what your life would have been like if you had not left the ministry, if you had stayed in the Congregational Church back in Cambridge?"

"I do not regret my decision to move up here to Fryeburg. However, the passing of time for a minister makes him wise. The passing of time for a farmer simply makes him old," he sighed wearily. He abruptly changed the subject. "That is a beautiful sight," James pointed to Sarah, Grace and Hannah laughing as they picked the apples using the long poles with small baskets attached at the end.

"How unusual," Hannah noticed the large ash basket into which the girls were throwing their bruised apples. "Why would anyone weave a red silk ribbon into a work basket?" she declared.

Grace stiffened as her cheeks blushed. "That is Mama's pretty basket," Libby explained. "She makes the prettiest baskets in the world."

Sarah intervened, "Grace has established quite a successful basket business. Her earnings have been greatly appreciated by the family."

"I believe a basket can be functional as well as beautiful." Grace responded.

"Is that not vanity?"

"It is most certainly not! I must tell you that God Himself is the author of all beauty. Why did He create flowers in their beautiful array of colors? He could have made them all brown. Is that vanity? Why did He create beautiful sunsets? He could have made the day turn immediately into darkness. Is that vanity? Look around you. There is beauty everywhere – the sky, the clouds, the flowers, the mountains. Is that vanity?"

"Truly, I have never looked at it that way before. I believe there is a difference between vanity and beauty."

Sarah breathed a sigh of relief. Would these two young women from such different backgrounds learn to become friends and sisters?

"Grace, I believe this is the most beautiful apple basket I have ever seen," Hannah complimented.

After an afternoon of working outdoors, everyone was hungry when they sat down at the Liberty Table that evening. In addition to their apple picking the three women made a plentiful meal. Grace made a kettle of winter vegetable soup with onions, celery, carrots, turnips and potatoes seasoned with sage, marjoram, parsley and savory.[1]

Sarah baked three-grain bread with cornmeal, rye flour and wheat flour.[2] During the war the family lived on corn bread. Wheat did not grow well in New England and had to be imported from the Mid-Atlantic States. Imported wheat was often not available during the revolution.[3] Because wheat was still expensive, Sarah often mixed it with cornmeal and rye.

Hannah made her favorite dessert called apple charlotte. She placed 8 slices of stale bread in a buttered baking dish and added 3 cups of sliced apples, warm milk, sugar and cinnamon. She baked it on a trivet in a Dutch oven.[4]

"Benjamin, I learned a profound lesson today," Hannah offered part-way through the meal. "There is a difference between beauty and vanity."

"I guess there is," Benjamin nodded as Grace smiled ever so slightly.

Sarah breathed a sigh of relief. Hannah was indeed a humble and gracious woman.

"I also learned a profound lesson today," Benjamin added. "I learned I can get more lessons planned and organized in one afternoon while picking pumpkins with my father than a week by myself in the classroom."

"Tomorrow you will learn another profound lesson in how to use my cider press," Ethan added.

Of all the building projects Ethan completed on the farm, the family's cider mill was his favorite. They would no longer need to depend on neighbors' apples and cider presses for their year's supply of cider. The maturity of their apple orchard coincided with the completion of the press. He envisioned many future cider-pressing parties and profits from selling apples and apple cider.

Ethan had studied and measured every cider press he could find in Fryeburg. Cider presses came in many sizes and styles; most were family owned, some small models were portable to serve an entire neighborhood. He was also aware that large, stationary presses served beverage businesses in larger towns and cities. It took him the major portion of two years to design and finally build a small, simple, yet efficient cider press built of local hardwood.

The first step in constructing the cider press was to make an apple crusher. The cider press would squeeze more juice, more efficiently, from smaller pieces of apples than from the entire fruit. Ethan made a wooden box-like structure that was nearly 15 inches long and 8 inches wide at the top but only 10 inches long and 4 inches wide at its tapered bottom. Within the box, about one-half of the way down, extending the entire length, he fitted a 4 inch wide wooden axle which he had turned from a small, straight section of firewood. He drove nails into the entire, smooth surface of log until it was studded with many uneven rows of nails driven into it all to the same height.

The interior surface of the tapered box was also covered with a triple row of nails, all similarly driven into the box's edge so that an even, 2 inches of all the nails was exposed. When a cranking handle was fastened to the end of the log that stuck out through the end of the box, the nail-studded axle could be turned within it. Any and all apples dropped into the box were forced against the nails driven into the sides of the box, which sliced through, fractured and broke them up into small, juice-laden sections.

The second step was to construct a sturdy frame, approximately twenty-eight inches wide and forty inches tall, to support the cider press. In the very center of the top cross-piece of the frame, he bored a vertical, three-quarter-inch hole through which he systematically and forcefully inserted a series of screw taps to create the spiraling threads that would perfectly accept the two-foot-long, one-inch-thick turnscrew he had ordered from a manufacturer in Boston. He attached a thirty-inch-long, maple handle to the top of the turn screw.

The most time-consuming project was building the two "leaky buckets". Ethan made them in the same manner as true wooden buckets, except that he drilled many holes in the bottom and left narrow gaps between the staves. Called 'baskets' by most cider makers, these would each hold a bushel of crushed apples. The final step was to make a circular, wooden plunger which would snuggly fit inside the leaky bucket. Turning the handle of the turnscrew slowly forced the plunger down into the awaiting bucket, or 'basket', compressing the apple pieces. Thick, pulpy, sweet-smelling apple juice flowed through the sides and the holes onto a gathering-tray and finally into a container beneath.

Libby and Sadie excitedly threw the dropped apples they had collected days before into the grinder while Benjamin turned the handle. Many very small apple chunks dropped into the bushel basket below. "It is working!" Libby squealed.

"Of course it is. Everything Uncle Ethan makes works," Sadie said proudly.

Micah dumped the crushed apples into the leaky bucket and Ethan slowly turned the handle of the turnscrew. As designed, fresh apple cider poured out through the holes and sides of the bucket, gathered into the tray and was diverted to the kettle below. The family continued the process all morning. By noon their first barrel was filled.

The ladies appeared with a ladle and eight cups. "This is the best cider in the whole world!" Libby exclaimed.

"Of course it is. Uncle Ethan made it," Sadie hugged him and then asked for a second cup.

Evenings and mornings grew colder while the afternoons remained pleasant. The men installed the three Franklin stoves in the fireplaces in the dining room, the drawing room and James and Sarah's bedroom.

Sarah and Hannah peeled and cored the apples before Grace sliced them and strung them on rugged homespun yarn across the kitchen by the hearth to dry. The root vegetables were harvested and stored in the cool, root cellar under the kitchen. Basil, rosemary, mint, oregano and thyme were picked, tied together and hung to dry.

The girls continued to pick up the apples that dropped on the ground; Ethan continued making cider.

The men stacked the last of the seasoned firewood in the new wood shed Micah had built attached to the back of the house.

After the first, hard frost arrived, James pronounced it was now time to butcher a hog. The weather had grown sufficiently cold to safely freeze the pork. Benjamin excused himself, stating it did not take four men to slaughter a pig and he would prepare some Latin lessons in the drawing room.

Although Grace had become an accomplished farmer's wife there were two jobs which she detested – making sausage and making soap. She did not relish the thought that the next couple of days would be devoted to these unpleasantries.

"Mrs. Miller, I have never made soap before. Mrs. Chase always sent me to the chandler shop to buy some. Would you be so kind as to teach me?" Hannah asked to Grace's relief.

"Perhaps Grace could be willing to make the sausage while we are outdoors making the soap," Sarah suggested. Ethan eagerly volunteered to help Grace.

Benjamin offered to help the ladies with the more cumbersome aspects of soap making as he started an open fire in the backyard and dragged the large kettle reserved for soap making out from the barn. "There are three basic steps in making soap," Sarah explained to her student. "First we must render the fat, secondly we make lye from wood ash and third we mix the fats and lye together." Sarah made everything she did sound simple. "Fat from cattle is called tallow which I use to make candles. Fat from pigs is called lard. We have a fresh supply of lard."

The two women placed the lard into the kettle with an equal amount of water and allowed the mixture to boil until all the fats had melted. After putting out the fire, they added more water and allowed the solution to cool down overnight.

"That was not too difficult," Hannah commented cheerfully.

"The fun shall begin tomorrow. Let us make a quantity of applesauce and a double batch of fried sausage, onions and potatoes for tonight and tomorrow."

After breakfast Sarah and Hannah headed for a small shed. "The next step is making lye from ash and water. This," she opened the door to reveal a wooden structure also built by Ethan "is our ash hopper. Throughout the year we shovel the ashes from our hearths and throw them into the top opening. We add water to keep a continuous supply of lye. As you see the lye drips from the bottom opening into the bucket below."

 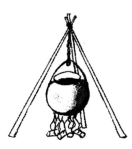

Once again Benjamin started an outdoor fire. The women returned to the kettle where the purified fat had solidified and floated to the top leaving the impurities in the water below. "Today we shall mix the rendered fat and the lye solution, boil and stir it for the next six hours until soap is formed. However, before we begin I must determine if the lye is of the correct strength." She grabbed the container under the ash hopper.

"How do we do that?" Hannah asked curiously.

"After twenty-five years of soap making, I made a discovery." She placed an egg in the lye solution, where it floated with an area about the size of nine-pence exposed above the surface. "Excellent," she smiled. "It is most vexing when the lye solution is too weak, then I must add more ashes. If it is too strong, then I must add more water.

I do not know how many batches of soap I have ruined before I learned this trick a few years ago."

"That is truly the strangest thing I have ever heard of. How does that work?"

The older woman laughed as she shook her head, "As Ethan often says, 'it works. Do not ask me why. It just works.'"

The women combined the lye with the fat and began to stir. "How shall we know when it is ready?"

"It is just like boiling maple sap. When it turns to syrup, you know."

"I have never made maple syrup. Truly I have much to learn."

"Dear, you will have the rest of your life to learn it."

Over six hours later Sarah stated with satisfaction, "It is done."

"This does not resemble the cakes of soap we purchased at the chandler."

"We are making soft soap. To make hard soap we would add common salt to the end of the boiling. As salt is rather expensive, I prefer to reserve it for food preservation and not waste it making cakes of soap. When the soap cools, Micah and Ethan will pour it into a barrel and store it in the pantry. Later we will ladle the soap out with a wooden dipper as we need it."[5]

The Millers enjoyed a bountiful meal to celebrate a successful harvest. Micah and Ethan shot a six-point buck on their second day of hunting. The aroma of roasting venison filled the house. Stewed beets, winter squash pudding, apple dumplings, cranberry sauce and hot mulled cider completed the meal.

The Millers and the good families of Fryeburg were prepared for the winter and the Preceptor was prepared to commence the first school year of Fryeburg Academy.

V

The Preceptor

"Grace, would Paul Revere and his kin like to make a donation to the Fryeburg Academy?" Benjamin asked sheepishly.

"That will depend upon what you wish for a donation."

"I wish to present each scholar with a new quill and a supply of ink. I have purchased several sticks of ink in Philadelphia. All I need to do is to add warm water and my class will have an ample supply. However, I find myself in need of fifty goose feathers."

The sounds of honking geese and shrieks of laughter brought Ethan, Micah and James out of the barn and into the barnyard. Libby and Sadie were rounding up the geese while Benjamin was struggling to hold onto an angry gander.

"Do you intend to just stand there and laugh or to help me?" a disheveled Benjamin asked in exasperation.

"I intend to stand and laugh," Ethan chuckled.

"Put that bird down before you strangle it!" Micah yelled.

"Papa, come help us," Libby giggled.

With the additional help of Micah, Ethan and James, Benjamin was supplied with sixty feathers by the end of the morning. He spent the next two days with the tedious task of cleaning, preparing and trimming each quill.

After heating the quills in hot ashes, he carefully scraped the barrels of each with the back of a blade to remove the external membrane. He further cleaned and polished each piece with a clean woolen cloth. With the sharpest knife in the kitchen he sliced off the tips on each end of the quills before placing them in a boiling solution of water, salt and alum for fifteen minutes. He carefully lined them up on a bench near the hearth to dry overnight.

It was to Benjamin's advantage the next morning dawned with freezing rains and bitter winds. James painfully limped to the Liberty Table for breakfast. "Father, could I entice you to spend a morning by the hearth engaging in political conversation and trimming quills?"

"My old bones and I thank you for the kind invitation," he smiled.

"It will take more than conversation to entice me to spend hours cutting quills," Ethan stated emphatically.

"How about apple-pumpkin cornbread?" Hannah offered.

"It is a deal. After breakfast I will retrieve some knives from the shop."

"Benjamin, I will gladly help in exchange for two quills and some ink," volunteered Grace, a prolific letter writer.

"I remember well the days I prepared and trimmed the quills when you boys were young. For a cup of tea and the pleasure of your company I will also help," Sarah smiled.

"We shall have a party!" Libby declared. "Papa, will you stay and help too?"

"It is only fair that Uncle Benjamin helped me during harvest, that I should lend him a hand today."

While Hannah, assisted by Libby and Sadie, mixed the batter and carefully placed the iron pot with its tightly sealed lid in the ashes to bake, the others began the task at hand. Each quill required two additional sloping cuts. Ethan volunteered to nick each point, called a nib, and split it before James and Benjamin took each square-cut nib and beveled them into the finished product.[1]

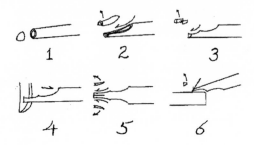

"Next year, your students are bringing their own quills to school," Ethan said as he took a bite from the warm corn bread.

Later that evening Benjamin carefully copied the "Rules and Regulations of Fryeburg Academy" that would be posted at the back of the classroom.

>   1. *Every scholar shall seasonally attend at the hour*
>   *when the Academy opens and, if the distance of*
>   *abode and other circumstances admit, before the*

entrance of the Preceptor, at whose entrance they shall rise up in their place.

2. *Every scholar shall behave with becoming solemnity and reverence at time of prayers as it behooves all who acknowledge a dependence on the supreme author and governor of the universe.*

3. *Decency in apparel and cleanliness of body are indispensably necessary as they promote health of body and vigor of mind.*

4. *Every scholar shall carefully avoid all immoral, profane and immodest discourse and conversation or any scurrilous or abusive language unbecoming the character of scholar and gentleman.*

5. *Decency of behavior and good manners shall be carefully observed by every scholar both at home and abroad.*

6. *No scholar shall habituate himself to the use of strong liquors or sit drinking at any house of public entertainment.*

7. *Each scholar shall in turn, at the direction of the Preceptor, prepare wood for and kindle the fire in season in the morning and sweep the house in the afternoon.*

8. *No scholar shall willfully break any window, glass or throw stones, snow balls or any other thing to endanger the same, nor deface or injure the building by cutting, scratching or any other way.*

9. *When school is dismissed every scholar shall retire in an orderly and decent manner and before the Preceptor leaves.*

10. *Every scholar convicted of profane language and swearing shall forfeit and pay one shilling for each and every crime of which he shall be convicted.*
11. *Every scholar convicted of playing cards shall pay one shilling for each offense.*
12. *Any scholar convicted of pilfering from his fellow students shall restore four fold.*
13. *Any scholar convicted of striking or abusing his fellow students shall be subject to a fine not exceeding ten shillings.*[2]

Tomorrow was opening day of the academy and Benjamin was growing anxious. Hannah found him seated at Grace's Chippendale desk frowning at the papers before him. She put her hand over his, "My dear, sweet Benjamin, do not be anxious. Remember the evenings you excitedly told me that the Constitution had been ratified. Remember your excitement when you explained the Bill of Rights to me. Take that excitement and joy and explain that to your students. I shall pray for you tomorrow."

"Hannah," Benjamin smiled gratefully, "I do not know what I would do without you."

"Uncle Benjamin, you look handsome," Sadie giggled at breakfast. Benjamin was wearing a fine, white, ruffled linen shift, a blue woolen waistcoat with pewter buttons which matched his blue woolen britches which buckled below the knee. White silk stockings contrasted with his black leather shoes with pewter buttons. His indigo, English frock coat had a turned-down collar and large cuffs.[3]

"You look like you are going to a funeral." Micah stated.

"No, you look like John Quincy Adams." teased Ethan. Benjamin spent much of his childhood jealous of the privileged son of John and Abigail Adams who attended boarding school in Paris, studied in Amsterdam, and accompanied Ambassador Francis Dana to Russia.

"Never mind your brothers," Sarah gave her two sons a warning glance, "you look dignified and professorial."

Hannah's smile warmed his heart as he grabbed his leather satchel filled with books and papers, left the house, waving to his giggling nieces who were standing in the window. He strode up the lane to Main Street and turned right onto the school property. As he briskly entered the classroom forty-eight young scholars stood at attention.

"Gentlemen, please be seated," Benjamin stated with authority as he stood behind his podium. "My name is Mr. Miller and I have the privilege of being the first preceptor of Fryeburg Academy as you all have the privilege of being the first students. Our first order of business shall be to take attendance."

He studied the room filled with boys as young as thirteen and young men as old as eighteen. Some were attired in their Sunday best for the first day of school while others wore clean but simple clothing befitting the life on a farm. The roster included familiar surnames such as Osgood, Dresser, Walker, Evans, Knight, Bradley and Wiley as well as names of the many newcomers to town.

"Please rise as we open the day with prayer." It was the preceptor's duty to pray publicly with the pupils[4] and Benjamin felt self-conscious. His father always prayed aloud at home, Reverend Fessenden prayed aloud in church and Benjamin was accustomed to praying silently. He took a deep breath, closed his eyes tightly trying to pretend he was alone in the room. "Our gracious Heavenly Father, the Creator of Heaven and Earth, we thank Thee for the privilege Thou hast bestowed upon us to study your Word and your world. Give us the wisdom and patience to diligently pursue our studies. Amen." His prayer was short yet sufficiently pious.

"Gentlemen, please be seated." He had prepared his first lecture with the same precision and intensity as he had prepared for previous opening statements in court. "What is education? Is it simply amassing facts and knowledge? What was the role of education in the American colonies? What was the role of education in the American Revolution? What is the role of education in our new republic? These are some of the questions we will seek to answer during the course of this year.

History records the fact that the Congregational churches of New England gave to this country its system of public schools; so the determination of our forefathers that their children should be able to read the Word of God and that pastors of their churches should be educated men, brought into being the free-school system of the country.[5] As early as 1647, New England Puritans required every township with fifty householders to appoint one within their town to teach all such children to write and read."[6]

Last year the inhabitants of Fryeburg, Brownfield and Conway, New Hampshire decided to establish a grammar school for the instruction of the youth in English, Latin and Greek languages and in such other branches of literature.[7] Fluency in reading and writing Latin is the minimum requirement for acceptance into college. Many text books, especially in law and theology are only printed in the classical languages.[8] Therefore, the mornings will be devoted to the study of languages and literature. In the afternoons we will study the laws and developments of our new nation. Democracy needs an educated populace to thrive."

One older student raised his hand, "Sir, I do not intend to go to Harvard. I plan to take over the family farm. Why do I need to learn Latin and Greek?"

"I am so glad you asked." Benjamin turned and began writing a series of words on the board - gregarious, congregate, congregation, segregate, integrate and aggregate. "What do these words mean? What do they have in common?" If you knew Latin then you would know that *gregis* means flock, herd, group, or company.

Gregarious means living in a group, fond of company or socially outgoing.

Congregate means to gather together in a group.

Congregation is a group of church goers gathered together.

Segregate means to separate a group while integrate means to bring in individuals from different groups into one group.

Aggregate means to gather in a lump or a sum."[9]

Then he turned back to the blackboard and wrote down theology, monotheism, polytheism, atheism, Pantheon, Dorothy and Theodore. "What do these words have in common?"

One student cautiously raised his hand. "All but one has the letters t-h-e-o in them."

"Very good. Can anyone tell me what those letters means? If you knew Greek you would know that *theos* means god.

Theology – *logos* is Greek for word or study plus *theos* for god and you put them together and have the study of god.

Monotheism – *mono* is Greek for one or alone plus *theos* for god and you put them together and have the belief in one god.

Polytheism – *poly* means many add *theos* and you have the belief in many gods.

Atheism – *a* or *ab* means away from in Greek. It means away from god or disbelief in god."[10]

"Sir, what do Dorothy and Theodore mean?"

"*Doron* in Greek means gift. Who can tell me what Dorothy means?

Several eager students raised their hands. "It means gift of god. Theodore also means gift of god."

"Sir, you forgot Pantheon."

"If I told you that *pan* means all in Greek, then what would Pantheon mean?"

"All gods?"

"Very good. The Pantheon is a temple in Rome built to worship all the Roman gods.[10] Gentlemen, that is why we shall be studying Greek and Latin," he smiled as he distributed books and began the class.

After lunch Benjamin began his government class. "Who is the President of the United States?" Everyone eagerly shot up their hands.

"George Washington."

"Who is the Vice-President?" Most of the students raised their hands.

"John Adams."

"Who is the Secretary of State?" Half of the students raised their hands.

"Thomas Jefferson."

"Who is the Secretary of the Treasury?" Only three students raised their hands.

"Remember the name Alexander Hamilton because he will impact your life and the lives of your children and grandchildren more than the other three men combined."

Benjamin smiled as he noticed that last statement piqued their interest. "Can anyone tell me what is the Coinage Act of 1792? In April of this year the United States Congress established the United States Mint and regulated the coinage of our country. It is also constructing a mint building in our nation's capital, Philadelphia."[11] He noticed a few looks of confusion. "A mint is a building which produces coins – not to be confused with the leaf with which we make our tea." A few chuckles were heard.

"This act establishes the American dollar as the unit of money and creates a decimal system for our currency."[12]

Several students raised their hands. "Sir, what is a dollar? What happened to our shillings?"

"Why did they do that? What is wrong with the money we have now?" a second student asked.

"Our nation has four serious problems with the way things are now. First, there is no common system of monetary accounting. Each state, as a colony, had created its own unit of account based on the British system of pounds, shillings and pence.

Secondly, the medium of exchange is the Spanish dollar, a silver coin. In addition a variety of coins – both gold and silver are currently being circulated. We need to establish a relationship between gold and silver. Finally all of these coins are foreign. A domestically produced coinage will be a hallmark of our independence."[13]

"Sir, what will happen to the money we have now?"

"The government will be minting and using the new coins soon. It will take years, perhaps a decade, for private citizens and businesses to gradually shift from pounds and shillings to dollars."[14] Benjamin wrote a large $ on the blackboard. This is the symbol for dollar."

"Sir, how many shillings is a dollar worth?"

"That is the wrong question to ask. Dollars measure the weight of standard gold or silver. Copy this chart I am writing on the board, for tomorrow there will be a test."

Eagles	$10.	17.5 g. standard gold
Half Eagles	$5.	8.75 g. standard gold
Quarter Eagles	$2.50	4.37 g. standard gold
Dollars	$1.00	27.0 g. standard silver
Half Dollars	$.50	13.5 g. standard silver
Quarter Dollars	$.25	6.74 g. standard silver
Dimes	$.10	2.70 g. standard silver
Half Dimes	$.05	1.35 g. standard silver
Cents	$.01	17.1 g. copper
Half Cents	$.005	8.55 g. copper [15]

Benjamin wrote the word "bimetallic" on the board. "This means of two metals. Our coinage system is bimetallic because it uses both gold and silver.

Gentlemen, I believe our time is up for the day. Remember there will be a test tomorrow on our new monetary system. Have a pleasant evening."

Sadie was the first to spy Benjamin returning up the lane. "Uncle Benjamin, I missed you." She hugged his leg. "Did you have a good day?"

He picked her up and said, "I had a very good day."

"Uncle Benjamin, tell us everything!" Libby pleaded as he and Sadie entered the back room where the ladies were busy carding and spinning wool.

"I will share my adventures tonight. Now I must change my clothes, bring in some water from the well and some wood from the woodshed. I must earn my keep around here," he winked at Hannah.

That evening Benjamin enjoyed the attention as much as the food.

"Father, do you think it will snow?" Benjamin anxiously asked one morning in late November as he watched the wind blowing the leafless branches against the dark, gray sky.

"We are overdue for a snow storm."

Benjamin put on his brown, woolen great coat and leather gloves.

"I am confident that today's lecture shall be thought provoking," Hannah encouraged. For the past five evenings the family had discussed Benjamin's "Ideas have Consequences" lecture. Libby and Sadie took their places by the window to wave to Uncle Benjamin as he walked to school. He grabbed his hat and his satchel and headed out the door.

He had grown quite fond of his students during the past six weeks. He now actually enjoyed praying aloud in class. He encouraged his students to ask questions and he arranged study groups with the gifted students helping the others with their Greek and Latin. His chronic shortage of paper and textbooks necessitated students working together and giving oral reports.

Some parents and some trustees were dubious of Benjamin's unorthodox teaching methods. He assured them that he was being a good steward of the academy's limited resources. Public speaking is an important skill which takes years of practice before becoming proficient.

Benjamin invited Reverend Fessenden, James Osgood and Moses Ames, members of the Board of Trustees, to observe the day's activities. He realized that as he would be evaluating his students, the trustees would be evaluating him.

His students rose to attention as Benjamin entered the classroom. "Mr. Wiley, thank you for the roaring fire this morning. I appreciate that you arrived extra early in order to provide comfort to your classmates and our esteemed visitors. Gentlemen, today we will set aside our language studies and devote our attention to the history of political thought. Today's lecture is entitled "Ideas have Consequences." When I write your assigned topic on the board, please have the spokesman of your study group come to the podium and lecture. Class, let me remind you that you are to give each speaker the same respect which you give to me. Feel free to ask questions. Be sure to take notes for you will be tested on this material. Let us begin.

Benjamin wrote on the board, *The Divine Right of Kings*. A trembling sixteen-year-old walked up to the podium. "The Divine Right of Kings is a Greco Roman political philosophy which maintained that the king was divinely appointed and therefore could dictate and enforce not only civil behavior, but also religious beliefs. Because God, rather than the people, selected him, everything the king required should be honored by the people as God's will. The King could not be restrained or punished by any earthly law."[16]

"What if the king was wrong? What if he was evil? Suppose the king commanded something against God's law?" someone asked.

"Sometimes people plotted to assassinate the king. Or, as in England, they had a Civil War where they beheaded King Charles I. The American colonies had a Revolution. King Louis in France is in jail right now."

"Very good. I liked the way you gave examples of when people disagree with the king," Benjamin complimented. "Can anyone in the class give me examples of kings commanding his divine rights?"

"People had no rights under the Pharaohs of Egypt," someone suggested.

"King Henry VIII broke away from the Catholic Church and became the head of the Church of England because the Pope would not let him divorce his wife," another continued.

"That is an excellent example of civil authority, the king, usurping religious authority. This brings us to..." Benjamin wrote on the board, *1075 Pope Gregory VII.*

Another student stood behind the podium. "Five hundred years before Henry VIII, Pope Gregory instituted sweeping reforms to free the Roman Catholic Church from the control of European political rulers. He redefined the limits of state power as well as the extent of individual rights."[17]

Upon seeing *The Magna Carta* written, another student explained that "The Magna Carta, Latin for the Great Charter, was written by Cardinal Stephen Langton, the Archbishop of Canterbury in 1215 which defined the legal rights of freemen in England. When Prince John was forced to sign it, he promised to protect the rights of the church, the rights of Christians and the rights of English citizens.

By the end of the 13th Century a group of Catholic lawyers called canon lawyers formulated the concept of 'inalienable rights' which means unchangeable, permanent and personal rights or rights of the person."[18]

A student raised his hand, "How is it that the Catholics are making these rules and not the Protestants?"

"This is back in the 1200's. Protestants were not invented yet," the spokesman replied.

Benjamin tried to keep a straight face. "This is why chronology is so important. Did someone else have a question?"

"I thought Thomas Jefferson invented 'inalienable rights'. In the Declaration of Independence we have inalienable rights of life, liberty and the pursuit of happiness," one student in the back row challenged.

The student behind the podium gave that comment some thought. "I guess he stole the idea from the Catholics."

"That was a good observation," Benjamin congratulated the nervous speaker who now gave a sigh of relief. "Class, this is an example of ideas having consequences. Mr. Jefferson, our esteemed Secretary of State and the author of the Declaration of Independence studied law at the College of William and Mary in Virginia where he studied the Divine Right of Kings, the Magana Carta and 12th century canon law just as you are today.

He took this information and applied it to the colonists' experience.

"Sir, may I ask you a question?" one student in the front row asked.

"How shall we learn, if we do not ask questions," Benjamin invited.

"Do slaves have inalienable rights?"

"Absolutely," Benjamin answered without hesitation. Some of the students looked uncomfortably around the room.

"But sir, slavery is legal."

"It is legal, but is it moral? Our inalienable rights were bestowed upon us when our Creator created man in His image. No government has the authority to rescind the very rights that God Himself has given us."

"Mr. Miller, what shall we do if we disagree with a law? Are you implying we should break the law?" Moses Ames challenged.

"An American citizen has two choices; he may break the law or he may change the law. I prefer the latter option. We will now move forward another three hundred years in our chronology of ideas. Perhaps it is time to 'invent the Protestants'."

A tall, lanky student walked to the podium as Benjamin looked out a window and noticed it had begun to snow. "The Protestant Reformation began in 1517 in Germany when a Catholic priest named Martin Luther challenged the Catholic Church. It was his intent to reform the church when he wrote his ninety-five theses, not to leave it. However, the Pope expelled him. His followers were called Protestants because they protested against the Catholic Church. They were also called Lutherans because they followed Luther."

"What does *sola fide* mean?" Benjamin asked.

"That is Latin for only faith. *Fide* is where we get our English word for fidelity or faithfulness. *Sola* is where we get our English word for solo or alone."

Benjamin smiled, "Someone has done his homework. Please continue."

"Luther believed it is only by faith in Christ that one enters Heaven whereas the Catholics at that time practiced indulgences or buying forgiveness from God by paying money to the Church. He also believed you should only believe in the Bible, *sola scriptura* which means only the Scriptures and not believe in extra Catholic writings."

"Excellent. Now please tell the class about Luther's political views."

"Luther insisted that the civil government had no authority to force people to believe any religious doctrine. He wrote an essay entitled "How Far Secular Authority Extends".[19]

"Was Luther attempting to protect the government from religion?"

"No, sir, he wanted to protect religion from the government. Kings and kingdoms shall all pass away but the Word of God remains true."

"That is very good. I see you were paying rapt attention to Reverend Fessenden's sermon on Sunday." Benjamin wrote on the board, *Calvin's Institutes of the Christian Religion.*

Another student stepped up. "John Calvin, a contemporary of Martin Luther, lived in Geneva,

Switzerland and shared many ideas of Luther's and wrote *The Institutes of the Christian Religion.*

Calvin believed in original sin, that men are sinners and would act badly toward others in society. Therefore society needs civil government to deal with bad conduct. The role of the state is limited to secular things. People's minds and beliefs are exempt from civil government control.

Calvin's *Institutes* includes a section called Calvin's Resistance Theory which states 'if a king requires any behavior offensive to God, resistance is not only permitted, it is demanded."[20]

"Well done. Who are the Huguenots?"

"They are French Calvinists."

"Who was John Knox?"

"John Knox was a disciple of Calvin who founded the Scottish Presbyterian Church."

"Ideas have consequences. Do not underestimate the influence of Calvin's *Institutes* upon the founding of our new nation."

"Sir, may I ask a question?"

"Always, Mr. Evans."

"I never heard of Calvin's *Institutes*. How can you be so sure that it influenced our nation's founding?"

"I assure you that every graduate of Harvard College, the College of William and Mary, Yale or the College of New Jersey read and studied *The Institutes*, in Latin may I add, before he could graduate. Men such as John Witherspoon, John Hancock, Samuel Adams, John Adams, Alexander Hamilton, Thomas Jefferson and James Madison would have studied these in college. In Fryeburg alone, Lt. Caleb Swan, Reverend Fessenden,

Dr. Emery, my father, James Miller and yours truly all studied these truths.

Benjamin wrote on the board *British Common Law* as he glanced outdoors and noted it was now snowing heavily.

Another student approached the podium. "The English legal tradition, called the Common Law, has ancient origins and is grounded in Judeo-Christian morality. In 890 A.D. King Alfred the Great had the laws of England codified. He simply took the Mosaic Law and expanded and modified it, applying it to the circumstances of the people of England at that time.[21.]

Over the centuries as new legal issues arose, the Common Law was expanded. Sir Edward Coke and Sir William Blackstone studied and clarified the Common Law and wrote law books." [22]

Benjamin asked, "Did our founders dispense with British Common Law in 1776?"

"No sir. On the contrary, they used the British Common Law as the basis of our own. Many of our Founders like John Adams, Thomas Jefferson or James Madison who studied law would have read Sir Blackstone's law books."

"Who followed the Common Law, Catholics or Protestants?"

The student looked panicked for a second, "Both?"

"That was a trick question. Yes. Both Catholics and Protestants found common ground in the British Common Law for it was founded on Biblical law and not sectarian ideology. It also provided a ground of consensus for our Founders back in 1776 as well as now.[23] Please continue with Mr. Blackstone."

"He said that the most important rights are God-given. They are not government-created."

Benjamin interrupted, "What term would you use to describe this idea?"

"Inalienable rights."

"Did Sir Blackstone originate this idea?"

"No, not at all, sir. The canon lawyers of the 13th Century did. Since he studied the British Common Law, he learned this idea and expounded upon it."

"Indeed. Ideas have consequences that will impact not just one generation but many generations to come. Before our esteemed Mr. Jefferson wrote the *Declaration of Independence* he wrote *Summary View of the Rights of British America* in 1774.

The final student stood behind the podium. "Jefferson states that society is built on two pillars, the law and rights. The two are inseparable and rest on a simple and powerful idea: the God who created nature, and who established a universal law called the law of nature, also created human beings, endowing each with inalienable rights. He agreed with the writings of Coke and Blackstone.

Man's life in society is governed and regulated by universal law, a moral code laid down by the Creator. This fundamental law is called the law of nature. The law of nature tells a person how to live justly with other persons, and it establishes certain rights that belong to everyone. These rights are attached to personhood itself: every human has those rights simply by being created.

Mr. Jefferson repeated these ideas in the opening sentences of the *Declaration of Independence*. Using the "laws of nature and nature's God" as the starting point, he proclaimed that "all men are created equal" and endowed by their Creator with certain inalienable rights including "life, liberty and the pursuit of happiness".[24]

"Well, done! Well done! What one believes will determine his actions. Ideas have consequences. Because I believe that this snow has the potential of becoming a storm, I will dismiss school an hour early to insure everyone will return home safely. Have a good weekend. I remind you that there will be a test on the material we covered today. Gentlemen, you are dismissed."

The trustees shook Benjamin's hand offering their congratulations. The young preceptor had passed his test.

VI

Family

Hannah did not merely observe the Millers; she studied them. She never knew one family could work so hard. Every member was a vital contributor to the success of the farm and the functioning of the home.

James Miller was a paradox. As a church elder and Fryeburg selectman, he was clearly a very influential man in town. As the head of the household, his family treated him with honor and respect. Yet he was not the "master" that she had witnessed during her childhood; he was a gentle and humble man. Townsfolk would stop by for his counsel and church members for his wisdom. He often invited new families in town for Sunday dinner.

An early riser, he accompanied Micah to the barn and worked until midmorning when he returned to rest in his favorite, wing-backed chair in the drawing room. It was obvious that the leg and hip he seriously injured in an accident a decade ago caused him discomfort on a good day and pain on a bad one. Sarah, who would have a pot of tea ready for his arrival, would often sit with him as he read the Scriptures aloud. Sometimes he would invite

Libby and Sadie to join him as he told stories from his childhood, or from Grace and Micah's childhood. He told them about the Mayflower's arrival at Plymouth carrying their ancestors John and Pricilla Alden on their mother's side and William Bradford on their father's side. He taught them the Westminster Catechism and Bible stories.

Sarah Miller was truly the example of the virtuous woman described in the Book of Proverbs, Chapter 31:

"A good wife, who can find?
She is far more precious than jewels,
The heart of her husband trusts in her,
And he will have no lack of gain.
She does him good, and not harm,
All the days of her life.
She seeks wool and flax,
And works with willing hands …"

Sarah made everything she did look effortless and treated Hannah like a daughter. In October Sarah took her best, black yarn and sat at her loom. "Winter will be here shortly," she warned, "and we must make you a proper winter cloak. I have some fine white wool that will make warm petticoats. I am thankful that you know how to knit, Hannah. Perhaps you could knit the girls and yourself some mittens and stockings.

"Mrs. Miller, what is that you are making?" Hannah asked one blustery, January afternoon.

"I hope it will be a hooked rug someday. I had baskets and baskets of woolen scraps for which I had to find a purpose. I took a loosely woven piece of linen upon which Grace drew this lovely design. I cut the scraps into narrow strips. Using a rug hook Ethan made for me, I hook the strips of wool through the linen," she demonstrated. "I use different colors to fill in the design."

"My, it is lovely. Look it is fields and mountains and clouds in the sky." Turning to Grace she smiled, "A rug can be beautiful as well as practical. Do you think I could learn to hook a rug? Grace, could you draw me a big white house with grass and bushes and sky?" Hannah spent hours with Sarah and Grace by the hearth hooking their rugs, sewing dresses with the new fabric purchased in Philadelphia, and knitting stockings.

The talk at the evening meal often turned to politics. Hannah was amazed when Sarah would eloquently offer her own insights and the men would respectfully listen. Nothing like this ever happened in the boarding house back in Philadelphia where the men would sit and talk for hours and the women remained in the kitchen where they cooked, scrubbed and toiled. Back in Virginia, she remembered the men were cloistered in one room with their brandy and tobacco and the women remained in another sipping tea and gossiping. Now she understood why Benjamin spent his evenings tutoring and discussing politics and court cases with her, for this is what his family did.

Strong, rugged and handsome Micah was a younger version of his father and the hardest worker of them all. Each year, the farm grew more productive as he raised and sold more livestock, plowed larger fields and planted more crops. He was not content to sit around indoors when there was so much to accomplish in his massive barn or outdoors in the fields.

Hannah found it interesting that such a big man was so quiet and soft spoken. He observed much and said little. He clearly adored his wife and daughters; his eyes would twinkle and his mouth would smile at the sight of each of them. Hannah often noticed his concern when Grace withdrew into one of her quiet moods or when she would silently slip away into her bedroom for a "moment's peace". The most she ever heard Micah speak was when he was disagreeing with Benjamin over politics.

One December evening James announced, "Our esteemed George Washington has been reelected for a second term"

"I fear we have discarded one King George only to acquire another," Benjamin lamented.

Micah put down his fork and turned to his brother in disbelief, "That was the most bizarre statement I have ever heard – even from you. What on earth do you mean by that, sir?"

"I simply mean that this nation's hero worship of George Washington has blinded them to the fact that there are more qualified men for the office."

"Such as that pompous Alexander Hamilton?" Micah challenged.

"No. I was thinking of our Vice President, John Adams. No one understands the law better than he. A graduate of Harvard, he has practiced law for decades, negotiated loans and treaties. Washington is an under-educated, slave-holding, soldier."

"There is more to leadership than mere knowledge," Micah contradicted.

"Such as?"

"Bravery for one. The ability to lead men under the most adverse and trying circumstances, for another. There is perseverance and humility as well. Where was your John Adams when Washington was at Valley Forge? Attending dinners in Paris, was he not?"

Benjamin was clearly agitated one February evening. "Please tell us what is upsetting you so," Sarah invited. "Did something happen at school today?"

"I have just learned that Congress enacted the Fugitive Slave Law.[1] It allows owners to retrieve a runaway slave in any state or territory. It also provides fines for those who interfere with the rendition process and preserves the master's rights to seek damages from those who knowingly helped fugitive slaves. This is an outrage! The federal government is interfering with states' rights. A state should have the right to ban slavery on their soil and to assist people in need. This federal law will supersede any state's law."

"Brother, what do you think of your federal government now?" Micah asked smugly. "Did I not warn you that the federal government will slowly take over the states?"

Benjamin bit his tongue, for he did not want to admit that Micah was right.

"I believe it is human nature that if you are of the same mind as the government, then you wish that government to have more power. Conversely, if you should disagree with the government, then you would wish for less power," Sarah observed.

"Trust me, once a government increases its powers, it will not voluntarily relinquish any of it," James warned.

Grace was not the superficial, insufferable, know-it-all child that Benjamin had described. Clearly, she was a refined, beautiful woman who appreciated beautiful things. She could turn a monotonous meal of reheated salt pork and baked beans into a feast by setting the dining room table with linens, china and silver. She was an adequate cook, more adept with assisting Sarah at the hearth than taking over by herself.

She was gifted with an artistic flair; adding ribbons to her baskets or making quilts a work of art rather than mere items for warmth. Hannah felt Grace's hooked rugs were too beautiful to step on. Although Hannah was an accomplished homemaker, she admired Grace's charm and style.

Grace was generous, even eager to have Hannah like her. "I must tell you these pewter buttons will look elegant, but not ostentatious, on your new black cloak. This was one of my favorite dresses but I have not been able to fit into it for years. I think it will look much better on you if you wish to wear it to church some Sunday."

One snowy afternoon Grace opened the trunk which held the fabrics Benjamin bought in Philadelphia. She held up a coral, flowered, cotton print and a bolt of solid coral fabric. "This will look lovely with your black hair, Hannah. I will make you a skirt and vest."

Hannah opened her mouth to protest.

"I assure you it will be a simple skirt and a simple vest with no lace or bows, silks or satins. You know that I am an only child, but I imagine this is the sort of thing sisters do for one another."

"I imagine that it is," Hannah agreed with a smile.

Grace knew how to make small talk with acquaintances and graciously handle any social situation. It was Grace who introduced Hannah to all the church ladies that first Sunday while Benjamin was busy shaking hands and being slapped on the back by the old timers.

After four months of observing Grace interacting with the ladies, Hannah found herself more comfortable in conversing with new acquaintances.

Yet, there were times Grace's eyes were filled with sorrow even when her face was smiling. Hannah understood the loss of the father you loved; she could not imagine the pain of losing a baby.

Ethan, the most handsome, eligible bachelor in Fryeburg, was impervious to the adoring glances by the many young women seeking his attentions. It was silently understood that he was building up his cabinet making business to ask for Nancy Colby's hand in marriage. Ethan was the first to smile, to laugh, to joke and whistled as he worked in his shop. His large hands were calloused and he always smelled like freshly cut wood. Free of the paternal burden of discipline, he would give his nieces piggy back rides from the barn and make them toys and games. He was the first to sit down at every meal and the last to get out of bed every morning.

During one of Benjamin and Micah's heated political exchanges, Micah turned to Ethan and asked, "What do you think?"

"I think if no one is going to eat the last biscuit, I will be happy to take it!"

He never complained, yet Hannah understood his frustrations with his business or the lack thereof. He crafted fine furniture made of black walnut, oak, cherry or white pine which the hard working folks of Fryeburg could not afford to buy. He was often kept busy repairing wagons, doing odd jobs or building coffins. He remembered Christmas Day of 1780 when he, his father and brothers lovingly built the coffin for his sister, Abigail, and felt it was an honor to provide this service to neighbors. A good-hearted man, he often did not charge grieving parents for child-sized coffins. Sometimes he would barter a coffin for a couple of apple pies or a day's help in chopping down trees. "I just do not know enough dead people to make a living," he lamented.

Mischievous, talkative Libby was her grandmother's helper and companion, efficiently carding fleece, rolling skeins of yarn into balls, sorting yarn into baskets by color. She was presently knitting her grandfather a lap blanket to keep "his old bones" warm while he sat in the drawing room. She listened to the adults' conversation during meals and would often ask Uncle Benjamin questions about politics during the evenings while he attempted to prepare lessons.

"Elizabeth, if only my students listened to me half as well as you," he smiled.

"Uncle Benjamin, I shall be your best student when I am at Fryeburg Academy."

"I am sorry to inform you that only boys may attend the Academy."

"I must tell you, I shall vote to change that law!"

"Libby, I am afraid that girls do not vote."

"Well, I shall take Mama's tea, throw it into the Saco and have a revolution!"

Even sweet, quiet Sadie faithfully performed her chores of feeding and watering the chickens and gathering the eggs. She visited and patted the livestock and updated her father with daily reports. Although timid with people, she had no fear of the horses and cows and spent much time with the sheep. However, her greatest joy was drawing. Because paper was a scarce commodity, Uncle Ethan would supply her with lumber scraps and worn-down pencil nubs for her to sketch animals, flowers, insects, and trees.

The Millers were often weary, regularly disagreed about politics but never theology, occasionally irritated one another but always expressed their gratitude for what they had. A sense of peace, acceptance and stability permeated their home. For the first time in her life, Hannah understood what it meant to be a family. For the first time in her life she truly felt loved and accepted.

VII

Hannah's Choice

B enjamin, who was focused on correcting Latin quizzes, did not hear Hannah enter the classroom that April afternoon. "Benjamin, may I have a word with you?"

"Hannah, I am so pleased to see you. It is not often the two of us have the opportunity to be alone," he stretched his arms out to embrace her.

"I know. I am here for I wish to speak with you privately. I have made my choice," she smiled radiantly as Benjamin's heart skipped a beat. "I have pondered and prayed for months and now I have chosen my freedom."

"Your. . . freedom." His face paled as he sat down on a nearby seat. "Why?" he almost whispered.

"Why? Because my Creator has endowed me with inalienable rights that no man has the right to deny! I am created in His image, just as you. Why should I be denied my freedom just because one ancestor arrived in this country in a slave ship? Am I less of a person than you are? Am I less of an American than you?"

"You speak the truth," he sighed as he placed a piece of paper in front of him and dipped his quill into the ink pot.

I, Benjamin James Miller, of the town of Fryeburg, in the Province of Maine, in the Commonwealth of Massachusetts hereby grant complete freedom to the slave Hannah Chase, formerly known as Royal Randolph, who was purchased by me from Mr. and Mrs. Henry Chase of Philadelphia on August 1, 1792, intending to convey any and all rights of free citizenship of these United States of America.
Benjamin James Miller, Esq.
April 2, 1793

He handed her the document.

"Benjamin, you kept your promise."

"A man is only as good as his word. Besides I could never break a promise to you," his voice cracked.

"I am free? I am truly free?" Tears streamed down her face. "I can now make my own choices?"

"My dear Hannah, you are free to make your own choices."

"Benjamin, why did you ask me to marry you?"

"Because, Hannah, I am lost without you. I would still be wandering the streets of Philadelphia looking for a bookstore without you. I could not have faced my first jury without you. I could not have faced my first class without you. I could not...I cannot. . ." he choked up.

"My sweet Benjamin, you are truly the most honorable man I have ever known." She took both of his hands into hers. "I, Hannah Chase, a free woman, have chosen you to be my husband and the father of my children. I want a small and private ceremony at home with your family."

"As long as we are married, it does not matter to me when and where!" He smiled.

Perhaps no one was more excited about setting the date and planning the wedding than Grace. "A wedding is just what this family needs. We have had too many funerals. We must pick the first Saturday in May after the close of school but before planting. First we must draw up the invitation list."

"I was planning to have a simple ceremony at home with just the family," Hannah explained.

"Hannah, not only are you marrying into one of Fryeburg's finest families, you are marrying the Preceptor of Fryeburg Academy. That comes with certain social obligations. His students and their parents, the church members, the Selectmen, the Board of Trustees shall all be slighted if they were not invited. I must tell you a lady and a wife must support her husband in his career."

"I fear that I do not know how to plan such an event."

"Mother and I will take care of the details. We would not expect you to know who to invite. A midafternoon ceremony would only require light refreshments of tea, cider and assorted cakes. Fortunately, the beginning of May is before blackfly season, and we can set up tables outdoors for the overflow of guests."

"Overflow of guests? What are black flies?"

"There is no time to make a dress. Come to the attic with me and let us see what we can find." picking up her skirts she dashed up the stairs in excitement. Benjamin shrugged and Micah gave her a grateful smile as she and Sarah followed Grace up the stairs.

Opening a large, wooden trunk Grace pulled out an elegant, ivory dress with flowing lace sleeves. This belonged to my mother. It is terribly impractical and hopelessly old fashioned."

"The ivory will look lovely with your black hair," Sarah encouraged as she held the dress up to Hannah.

"It is the most beautiful dress I have ever seen," Hannah whispered. "I fear it is much too ostentatious for a poor Quaker girl from Philadelphia." Glancing at Grace, she added, "However, it is truly fitting for the bride of the Preceptor of Fryeburg Academy."

"This is my wedding gift to you."

Hannah's eyes brimmed with tears. "Truly, no one ever gave me such a beautiful gift. I do not know how to thank you."

Grace slipped her arm through Hannah's. "You will be the most beautiful bride Fryeburg has ever seen!"

"I only wish to be the most beautiful bride Benjamin has ever seen," she blushed.

"The girls will need new dresses," Grace declared.

"I shall sew the dresses while the two of you write out the invitations. Ethan will deliver them," Sarah suggested.

Tonight we shall count the cups and plates. We may need to borrow some from Abigail Osgood. She always entertains a crowd and …"

Hannah learned that day not even free women always have the last word in their choices.

The night before the wedding, James called Benjamin into the drawing room. "Have a seat, son for I wish to have a private word with you on the eve of your wedding."

Benjamin blushed, "Father, I grew up on a farm. I know how babies are made."

James tried not to smile, "I am sure you do. A husband has numerous obligations – some more pleasant than others. Thus far in your life you have made decisions that only have affected you. That is all about to change tomorrow. It is an awesome responsibility to become a husband. The Lord will hold you responsible for your decisions and how they impact your family."

"I thought the husband is supposed to make all the decisions," Benjamin countered.

"A wise husband will confer with his wife before making those decisions. On many occasions your mother offered words of wisdom at times when I needed guidance.

After tomorrow your world must expand beyond your books and studies. Raising a family is like raising crops. First you must sow seeds of love and mutual respect and diligently water them with kindness and consideration. There will be times of drought and raging storms, but only the farmer who perseveres without wavering will have a harvest."

"Sir, did you use this metaphor with Micah?"

"Indeed. Perhaps it was more appropriate then?" James smiled.

Benjamin proposed, "A good attorney puts the needs of his client before his. He is the advocate and the protector from injustice. It does not matter how smart the attorney may be, if he fails to win the case for his client. Because it is the client who pays for the mistakes of the attorney, he must be wise and diligent and prepared in all matters. A good attorney realizes that the Judge is always watching, and he must follow the Judge's rules or be held in contempt of court."

"I see that you will take your vows seriously," James noted with approval.

"It is a solemn decision to become a husband."

The kitchen was bustling with activity. Grace was making the syllabub. She mixed 10 cups of fresh cream, 3 cups sugar and the rind of 6 large lemons in a large bowl. In another bowl she combined 4 cups of white wine, two cups of cream sherry and the juice of the lemons. She very slowly beat this into the cream mixture and whipped the ingredients until the syllabub was light and frothy. She covered the 6 quarts of mixture and Micah brought it down to the root cellar to chill overnight and to allow the flavors to ripen.[1]

Sarah was baking a wedding cake using her mother's recipe. "This is the same cake we had at my wedding," she smiled at Hannah. She had soaked 2 pounds of raisins in a cup of brandy the night before. Now she sifted 12 cups of wheat flour and added 4 tablespoons of mace, 2 tablespoons of grated nutmeg and 4 pounds of currants. After creaming 3 pounds of butter with 6 cups of sugar, she added 2 dozen eggs one at a time. She stirred in ½ cup molasses and the brandy that was not absorbed by the raisins. Finally she stirred in the sifted flour with the spices and fruit. She poured the batter into three greased pottery baking pans of different sizes and placed them in the preheated Dutch oven to bake for 2 ½ hours.[2] The day before, Hannah and Sarah made 6 dozen doughnuts and stored them in the pantry.

On the far end of the Liberty Table, Hannah was making soft gingerbread. She sifted 6 tea cups of flour and added 1 tablespoon of ginger and 1 tablespoon of saleratus.[3] She cut and blended 1 tea cup of butter and stirred in 1 tea cup of cream and 3 tea cups of molasses then poured the batter into greased cast iron pans to bake for forty-five minutes.[4]

Ethan was outdoors in the twilight setting up saw horses and planks in the back yard. Tomorrow, Grace would transform these into banquet tables covered with linens, china and bouquets of forsythia. Micah was upstairs attempting to put his overly excited daughters to bed.

"Yes, Libby, your dress is the most beautiful dress in the world. No, Libby, you may not sleep in it tonight!"

The tall clock in the drawing room struck 11:00 before the adults fell into bed.

The Congregational Church was packed with eager guests. "I cannot believe our little Benjamin is finally getting married," Mrs. Fessenden sighed.

"She is a pretty girl although not beautiful like Grace," Mrs. Dresser commented.

"She is pretty enough," Mrs. Evans countered. "I understand Quakers do not abide by outward appearances."

"Charm is deceitful, and beauty is vain, but a woman who fears the Lord is to be praised," Mrs. Fessenden quoted Proverbs 31:30.

"She is not very friendly," Mrs. Walker observed.

"Well, compared to Grace she appears quiet. But Micah needed an extroverted wife. Look how he has come out of his shell the past few years. Hannah is reserved and dignified. She will make a fine Preceptor's wife."

"It is a pity that her family will not be attending," Mrs. Ames added.

"I understand the poor thing lost her parents during the war."

A nervous Benjamin appeared at the front of the church with his two brothers by his side. As the violin music began, Libby and Sadie dressed in their matching blue and white flowered dresses walked down the aisle holding hands followed by Grace in a blue silk open gown.

Benjamin, turning pale, thought he might faint as he watched a radiant Hannah float down the aisle like an angel with her black curls piled high upon her head. Reverend Fessenden smiled at him reassuringly and whispered, "Take a deep breath and relax. You will be fine."

Second only to Abigail Osgood, Grace Peabody Miller was the finest hostesses in Fryeburg. The drawing room was filled with older men who surrounded James drinking syllabub and eating gingerbread. Sarah quietly observed Grace serving tea from a porcelain tea set her father had brought home from China and entertaining the younger women with Hannah at the center.

In the foyer, Benjamin was talking with Reverend Fessenden. Some of his students talked with their parents as they drank cider served from a crystal punch bowl. Other students sat on the steps of the grand staircase balancing a plate of doughnuts on one knee while sipping their cider from elegant wine glasses.

Sarah slipped outdoors where the three-tiered wedding cake sat in the middle of one of the banquet tables. Guests sat at the other tables eating cake and drinking cider or syllabub. Micah was discussing crops with the younger men as numerous children ran, played and laughed in the door yard. Where was Sadie? Sarah knew her shy granddaughter did not enjoy playing with large groups of children. Perhaps she was taking refuge in her upstairs bedroom. She quickly reentered the house through the back door and climbed the back stairway.

"Sadie!" she called over the din of conversation and laughter below as she first entered Ethan's room, then the girls' bedroom with their matching beds and quilts, the empty nursery and finally Grace and Micah's room. She looked in closets and under beds and she repeated Sadie's name.

Sarah stared out the bedroom window looking west to the Saco River hoping to find Sadie romping through the meadow by herself far from the noisy crowd. She swallowed the rising panic in her throat, "She's hiding in the sheep pen," Sarah whispered to herself.

She slipped into the barn unnoticed by the guests and called for Sadie in the sheep pen, the horse stalls, the oxen stalls and the hen house. She entered Ethan's shop hoping to find her granddaughter contently drawing pictures on scraps of discarded wood. "Mother, may I help you find something?" Ethan startled her.

"Have you seen Sadie? I cannot find her anywhere."

"Did you look under her bed?"

"Yes, I looked under her bed, your bed, every closet, nook and cranny and she is nowhere. Please help me find her before Grace misses her and becomes concerned."

Ethan casually sauntered to the frolicking children and asked, "Has anyone seen Sadie?"

"She was acting like a baby and did not want to play with us," Libby explained indifferently. "She went that way," she pointed toward the river.

"She is not in the meadow or I would have seen her from the upstairs window," Sarah quietly explained to Ethan.

"Perhaps she decided to chase a chipmunk into the woods. You know how children are," Ethan grinned for as a child he was notorious for tracking animals in the woods for hours without asking permission from his parents to leave the yard. "Let us walk towards the river and if we do not find her in the meadow, I will search the woods up river and you search down river. It will be hours before dark and I am sure she will return when she gets hungry. I always did."

Micah thought it was odd that his mother would leave her guests to walk through the meadow with Ethan. He went sprinting over to them. "Mother, what are you doing out here?"

"Micah, have you see Sadie?"

"No. Is she not with her mother?"

"I suspect she is seeking solitude from the crowd in the quiet of the woods, for I cannot find her anywhere in the house, the barn or the yard," Sarah failed in her attempt to mask her concern.

"Sadie! Sadie!" Micah shouted as he ran toward the river. Sarah prayed that Grace would not hear his shouting. He stopped two yards before the river as he discovered his daughter laying on her back motionless in the grass staring up at the sky. "Sadie! You answer me when I call you!" he scolded. "Sadie, did you hear what I said? Sarah Alden Miller! What is wrong? Answer me, Sadie!" Micah now stood over his daughter.

"Papa!" She sat up and smiled. "What a surprise! Did you come to get away from the crowd too?"

"Sadie, what are you doing out here by yourself?"

"Look at the clouds, Papa. I wonder how God created all those shades of white."

Micah sat down on the grass beside her as she turned her attention back to the clouds.

"Sadie," he said softly, "Why did you not answer me when I called?"

After moments of silence Micah bit his lip and swallowed hard. He realized that his daughter could not hear him.

VIII

Little Millers

R iverview Farm was filled with anticipation one late October morning as seven-year- old Libby was ready for her first day at the village school. Libby wore the new dress Grace had sewn of blue and white print fabric for the wedding. Her braids were adorned with blue silk ribbons.

The night before, Limbo had arrived with a gift of a black woolen bag with the letter "L" embroidered on the front. In it was a slate and chalk. "I thought our new scholar might need this tomorrow morning," Limbo smiled.

"Limbo, you kept this after all these years?" Benjamin asked. Turning to Libby he explained, "Your Aunt Abigail made this bag for him a long time ago."

This morning the bag also held her lunch of cornbread, cheese and an apple.

Micah took her hand, "Are you ready?" Grace had intended to walk her daughter to school, but she was exhausted and nauseous as she was with each of her pregnancies. Libby had insisted she was a big girl and could walk the mile by herself. However, Micah explained that it was his solemn, paternal duty and his honor to escort her.

"Remember, Elizabeth, do not interrupt your teacher and remain silent until you are spoken to," Grace lectured while holding back tears. "I cannot believe my baby is going to school."

"Mama, I shall be back this afternoon. Sadie shall keep you company," she kissed her mother and grandmother goodbye one last time before leaving.

Benjamin was grateful that his pregnant wife was not nauseous and overemotional like Grace as he kissed Hannah goodbye and ran out the door headed for the Academy.

That evening, as the family sat around the Liberty Table eating their meal, James asked his granddaughter, "Libby, please tell us what did you learn during your first day of school?"

Finally she could tell the family about her triumphant day. "Well, sir, the first thing I learned was that no one else in school knew that silk is made in China, or that Marco Polo brought back silk, venetian blinds and other treasures through the Silk Route to Venice. Sadly, no one had heard of Venice or Amsterdam for that matter. No one, not even the teacher, owns a copy of *The Merchant of Venice*. I told my teacher if he asked Mama, he might borrow her copy. I have the best penmanship in the class and I am already reading in the third reader. My teacher says in all his years he has never met such an egotistical seven-year-old!"

Benjamin stifled a laugh. "Libby, do you know what egotistical means?" James asked.

"No, Sir. But it must mean something good because Papa says Uncle Benjamin is egotistical."

Micah blushed; Benjamin bit his tongue; and Ethan roared with laughter.

The March winds rattled the windows of the school house as Benjamin debated if he should pack up his books and head for home while there were still moments of daylight. The comfort of the fire blazing in the Franklin stove in the drawing room was tempting after spending a day in the drafty classroom. Yet he savored the solitude which the late afternoons afforded. Life at Riverview Farm could be noisy and distracting.

He smiled as he heard Libby's giggles and Ethan's trudging footsteps up the wooden stairs. The door burst open with Libby declaring, "Uncle Benjamin, I could not wait a minute longer!" followed by Ethan holding a tin lantern with his right hand and carrying Sadie on his back. "Uncle Benjamin, we have a baby brother!" Libby squealed.

"Congratulations! Your Papa and Mama must be thrilled."

Ethan gently placed Sadie down. "He is an ugly baby," she stated seriously.

"He's fat and bald and red and blotchy and cries real loud," Libby elaborated. "Mama says he is beautiful. But I think she is sadly mistaken."

Ethan and Benjamin laughed out loud. "Girls," admonished Benjamin, "most newborns are not very attractive. They become adorable in the days and weeks ahead."

"Baby Jacob is already beautiful." Libby began.

"What!" Benjamin turned to a grinning Ethan.

"We have a new cousin!" Sadie announced.

"What? What! Ethan?"

"Benjamin, you are a father. It is a boy."

"It is too soon! Hannah? Is she faring well? The baby? It is too soon!" Benjamin stood up quickly.

"Mother says that he is little but just perfect."

Benjamin ran out the door leaving his cloak, his books and the key to the school house on his desk.

Benjamin ran panting into the front foyer calling, "Hannah!"

"Hush," Sarah scolded. "You will wake up the babies. Now come and meet your son," she took him by the hand and led him to the bedroom."

"Hannah, are you well?" he asked with concern as he gingerly sat at the edge of their bed.

"I am tired but so happy. Let me introduce you to Jacob Freeman Miller. Our son is a free man, Benjamin." Hannah smiled knowingly

"I think Freeman is a grand middle name. We were all born British subjects, but this generation is born as American citizens," Sarah continued.

"I concur whole heartedly," Benjamin agreed, "Freeman is a grand middle name."

"He looks just like a Bradford," Sarah pronounced. "Look at that head of black wavy hair," Sarah handed the tightly swaddled newborn to her son.

Benjamin held his child to his chest and cried.

The tall clock in the drawing room struck eight. The men were famished, yet dared not complain that there was no evening meal. Ethan was upstairs entertaining Libby and Sadie who were simply too excited to sleep. Sarah was upstairs with Grace as Hannah dozed fitfully down the hall. Grandfather, two fathers and two infants quietly sat around the hearth. Micah calmly held Alden James in his two large hands with the assurance of an experienced father. Benjamin awkwardly held Jacob terrified that he might drop him.

"Well sons, this has been quite the day. Relax, Benjamin. If you think holding one newborn is frightening, try holding two.

The day you and Abigail were born was the most terrifying one in my life! It was different when Micah was born. We were still living in Cambridge and Aunt Esther was there for the birth. But now we were here far from family. The original plan was that I was to bring Micah to Mrs. Osgood's home for her to watch him and then go pick up Mrs. Swan to help your mother. Of course Dr. Emery was nearby if we needed him.

It was one of the worst blizzards I had ever experienced. It snowed for three days. It was not safe for me to take three-year-old Micah out in that weather with no guarantee that if I left the house I would be able to return. I could not leave your mother alone."

Benjamin had never heard this story. "What did you do?"

"I delivered the two of you myself. It was a quick and easy delivery for you were much smaller than Jacob. I proudly swaddled you and handed you back to your mother. You did not even cry – it was more like a little whimper. Our joy and relief was short lived for Abigail was born minutes later. She was so tiny, so frail, ghostly white and her lips were blue. I feared that she would die within the hour.

The house was cold. I wrapped little Micah up in blankets, picked him up from his trundle bed and placed him in our bed with your mother. I swaddled the two of you together, placed you against my chest under my shift, threw on my great coat and spent the night pacing in front of this hearth. Of course I hadn't built the Liberty Table yet and there was plenty of room to pace.

I prayed aloud that the Lord would spare your lives, sang hymns and quoted Scripture. If it was God's will for my two children to die, then they would die knowing their father's voice, feeling his heart beating and hearing the Word of God." James sniffed as he wiped the tears from his eyes.

It was evident that Micah had heard this story before. Benjamin tried to imagine his father as a young, frightened father. He had only known him to be a wise, strong, capable man. Benjamin had always respected his father. That night he loved him.

"Micah, I am glad you have a son," Benjamin chose his words carefully. "I have only been a father for six hours and I could not imagine – I mean I am so sorry about the loss of William. I do not know how you managed."

"William was a healthy two-month old. Grace put him in his cradle that night and in the early morning he was gone. Dr. Emery said sometimes babies die suddenly like that. Father supported me and I in turn supported Grace and the girls through the ordeal. A man has to support his family."

Benjamin had always loved his brother. That night he respected him.

Riverview Farm was not prepared for the joys and exasperations that lay ahead. If Jacob woke up crying, Alden woke up screaming. If Jacob was rescued as he crawled toward the chamber pot, Alden was there to spill it. When pulling up to stand for the first time, Alden grabbed the tablecloth resulting in dishes crashing to the floor. Jacob contently sat there eating the maple sugar off the floor. Alden learned to walk first, Jacob followed six weeks later.

Micah built gates at the bottom and the top of both staircases. Yet the days were filled with bumps and bruises, squeals and squalls. Where ever the chubby, red headed, blue- eyed Alden went, the petite brown- eyed Jacob with a head of black curly hair followed three steps behind. They would cry whenever they were separated.

Micah enjoyed farming for the routine and predictability. A farmer knew what to expect each season; winter was for cutting firewood and making repairs; spring brought maple syrup and April showers followed by planting; summers meant long days of working sunup to sunset to prepare for the harvest. Children were so unpredictable! How did his father ever manage running a farm by himself while raising four children?

Benjamin enjoyed the life of a scholar for its solitude and quiet. An attorney had time to prepare by himself before defending his client before a jury. A teacher had time to study before interacting with his students in the classroom. Children were so noisy! How did his father ever find the time to read and meditate on his beloved Scriptures while raising four children?

One afternoon nearly ended in a tragedy. Ethan entered the kitchen looking for some cornbread in the pantry to "hold him over" until the evening meal. Hannah was churning butter at the far end of the Liberty Table while Grace was placing an iron pot in some coals. Jacob lost his balance, knocking Alden over. Ethan jumped over the table, spilling cream onto the floor and grabbed Alden with his right hand just before the toddler could fall head first into the flames.

The sounds of screaming mothers and crying babies sent Micah running from the barn. Micah silently listened to Ethan's explanation of events then turned back to the barn. Two hours later he and Ethan returned to the kitchen with a "baby pen".

"You would place our child in a pen like a litter of piglets?" Grace demanded.

"Pens are built to protect livestock. Is not our son more valuable than livestock? I have lost one son, and I will not lose another. A man must protect his family."

"Micah, I believe this invention to be a God-send. My husband shall thank you for your ingenuity when he returns from the Academy. But I shall thank you now."

"My mother never placed me in a "cage"," Grace argued.

"Your mother had a governess and six servants," Micah countered.

"Your mother had twins and she never put them in a pen."

"I do not remember Benjamin and Abigail being as active and aggressive as these two little men."

"Tis true," Ethan joked. "When Benjamin was their age, he was already reading the *Iliad* in Greek and Abigail was carding fleece and spinning and weaving."

"Ethan, the Lord has blessed us with your sense of humor and Micah's good judgment," Hannah smiled at her brothers-in-law. "I believe Alden shall be quite content if he is accompanied by Jacob in here."

One March afternoon, James entered Ethan's workshop shaking his head, "Remember when we thought the house was too big and we closed off several rooms for the winter? When did it get to be so small?"

"It will feel smaller next month when Hannah delivers her baby," Ethan smiled knowingly.

It was an unusually warm April afternoon. The snow was melting rapidly, the Saco River was rising quickly and mud season was at its apex. Benjamin's students eagerly left the school that afternoon to enjoy the sunshine on their walk home. He packed his books into his leather satchel, walked out the door, locked it with his large, brass key and headed down the steps.

"Uncle Benjamin! Uncle Benjamin!" Libby came running with Ethan several paces behind holding Sadie's hand.

Benjamin's heart pounded wildly, Ethan smiled broadly and Libby shouted, "It is a girl!"

Abigail Bradford Miller was born on April 24, 1796.

"Blessed chaos" is what James good naturedly described their household - crops, livestock, woodworking, four hungry men, three busy women, two giggling girls, two mischievous toddlers and one crying, six-month-old infant. This morning, Sadie's first day of school, was more "blessed" than usual.

"Are you ready, Sadie?" Micah asked as he headed out the door.

Sadie, who did not hear him, did not follow.

"Micah, be sure to tell the teacher, she needs to sit in the front row, so she can see the teacher clearly and hear what is being said," Grace reminded anxiously. "Libby, be sure to keep a close eye on your sister and hold her hand when you walk home from school."

At first Grace had not accepted Micah's opinion that Sadie was almost deaf. "That is ridiculous. Everyone knows that deaf children do not speak. Sadie learned to speak just as Libby did," she argued.

"Perhaps she was born with good hearing and is gradually losing it. I cannot explain how or why it is, but she hears nothing from the left ear and a little from the right. Have you not noticed if she looks right at you when you speak, she understands; yet if she is not looking at you, she does not hear you?"

"Many young children do not pay attention," Grace argued. "There is nothing wrong with Libby's hearing and she often does not pay attention."

That evening Grace quietly entered the kitchen where Sadie sat alone at the Liberty Table drawing pictures on a slate. She stood by her daughter's left side and smashed a cracked tea cup on the floor. There was no response.

"Grace, do not worry. Everything will be fine," Micah reassured his wife as he took Sadie's hand, looked into her eyes and clearly spoke, "Sadie, it is time to leave for school."

Sadie picked up her new brown woolen bag with the letter "S" embroidered in green, packed with a slate, chalk and her lunch.

"Mercy!" Sarah exclaimed as Libby returned home from school that afternoon with grass stains on her apron and her hair hanging loosely from her disheveled pig tails. "Did you have an accident?"

"No, Ma'am. It was not an accident – I did it on purpose." Sadie threw her bag on the table and headed up the stairs. "Sadie!" Sarah called after the dejected child, but Sadie did not hear.

"Tell us what happened." Grace asked with concern just as Micah emerged from the barn.

"Papa, a man has to protect his family. I did what I had to do."

"You had to protect Sadie?"

"Yes, Sir. The children were calling her stupid and bad names I cannot say."

Grace's cheeks burned with indignation. "Where was the teacher?" she demanded.

"He did not come out for recess. He is mean, he took Sadie's slate away because she was drawing and not listening."

"Micah, did you not request that Sadie sit in the front?"

"It does not matter, Mama. The teacher walks around the classroom when he talks. And when Sadie turned in her seat to watch him, he scolded her for fidgeting!"

"That is unacceptable! I am going to march over there first thing in the morning and pull her out of school." exclaimed a badly shaken Grace.

Micah looked angry but calmly responded, "Millers are not quitters. I will speak to him in the morning. He is equally responsible for the discipline of his charges in the school yard as well as the classroom."

"Micah, I disagree. A common school, indeed. Sadie is no common child! You and I never went to some common school. There is no law requiring us to send her. I fail to understand how that ignorant, unrefined man was offered a teaching position in the first place!"

"I will handle it, Grace."

Grace never knew what her husband said the next morning, nor did she realize that he stayed and observed through a side window. James and Ethan never told her that every morning around 10 o'clock he would silently slip away from the farm and walk to the school. Through the side window he watched Sadie nervously chew on her braid and swing her dangling legs as she stared straight ahead. The teacher continued to roam around the room.

One cold November morning, Sadie stared out a window and sketched the trees in her line of vision. She did not hear the teacher call her name or walk up to her seat. "What is the meaning of this?" he roared as he grabbed the slate.

Sadie Miller did not hear the squeaky hinge as the back door slowly opened or her father's footsteps as he slowly walked down the aisle toward his daughter's seat. The children sat still in their seats, wide-eyed with surprise. Mr. Miller was a very large man and the teacher was not. He nervously took three steps back as Micah knelt in front of Sadie. Looking into his daughter's eyes he calmly said, "I have come to take you home." Holding Sadie's hand he turned to the teacher and softly stated, "I believe you owe her an apology and you will return her slate and chalk to me now."

Libby stood up believing her father had come for her as well. "Please be seated, Elizabeth. You will be remaining for the rest of the year."

"Sadie? Micah?" Grace asked in surprise. "What are you doing here?"

"Papa rescued me!" Sadie sat down wearily.

"I told you I would handle it. I believe it is in the best interest of our daughter that we educate her at home. She can learn to read and write like any other child, if she is given the time and attention."

Sadie hugged her father in gratitude.

The Cabinet Maker

"Grace?" Ethan looked up from his tools with surprise for his sister-in-law rarely entered his workshop. She disdained getting wood shavings and saw dust on the hems of her petticoats.

"Ethan, I need some paint."

"I have some red paint pigment left over from the barn."

"That is a beginning. However, I want every color in the rainbow."

He put down his tools and simply stated, "Grace you are being unreasonable. I have much work to do and I cannot stop everything just because you have a notion you would like some paint."

Ethan Miller was rapidly becoming a popular man in town. In 1795, the town voted to build a second meeting house in the village. The congregation had outgrown the building; the population of the village had grown so they wanted to have their own church nearby and not travel north to the center of town. Ethan was hired to design and make the pews for the South Meeting House.[1] Located at the junction of the Main Road and the Mill Road, it was a large two storied building with two rows of windows and a gallery on three sides. The pulpit was set high on pillars, well above the congregation.[2] Ethan believed it was a vast improvement over the days when families met in Isaac Abbott's home in the winter because the first meeting house had no heat.

James had given Benjamin two acres of land at the corner of the Main Road and River Street for a wedding gift. When he and Hannah learned that they were expecting their second child, Benjamin hired Ethan to design and build his home as well as all the furniture.

He spent every waking minute drawing and revising plans, designing and redesigning the timber frame, selecting the finest white pines in the forest and subcontracting the making of the shingles, the clapboards and the lumber to local mills. He was still seeking bids on granite from nearby Conway for the foundation. To complicate matters, Benjamin insisted on paying the bills with those confounded eagles and dollars which no one in Fryeburg appeared to want.

This was his opportunity to earn some hard currency, to establish his business and reputation so he could ask for Nancy Colby's hand in marriage. He had no intentions to stop what he was doing so Grace could have some paint.

"It is not for me. It is for Sadie," she continued.

"Sadie?"

"Yes. She is fascinated by color – the shades of green in the plants, the shades of blue in the sky, the shades of brown of the earth. Art is an important part of her education. I thought you could teach the two of us how to make and mix paints of every color of the rainbow. I would never disturb you if it was only for me, but it is for Sadie," she smiled.

"Well, since it is for Sadie. I think I could spend some time tomorrow teaching her what little I know about paint. But it will cost you," he teased.

"I know pumpkin pie with whipped cream and cinnamon," she laughed.

"My own pumpkin pie," he corrected her. "I am not sharing it with my brothers."

Sadie quickly performed her morning chores and eagerly sat down with Uncle Ethan at the Liberty Table for her paint lesson.

"You need two things to make paint: pigment and vehicle." He noticed Sadie's look of confusion. "Pigment is usually finely ground minerals in different colors. Vehicle is something wet you add to the powder like linseed oil.[3] When I made the red paint for the barn, I grounded iron-oxide; you know rust, with a mortar and pestle and then added linseed oil a little at a time until I got the right consistency. Making paint is like making maple syrup or soap; it takes experience to know when it is the right thickness.

Lead white is the pigment for making white. Strips of lead are placed in earthenware pots and covered with warm, decomposing horse manure."[4]

"I must tell you that is disgusting!" Grace gasped.

"We have no shortage of horse manure," Sadie giggled.

"I do not understand why it works but it creates white flakes, which you grind to make the pigment and then add linseed oil. Making black is a little more pleasant. You mix bone black with linseed oil.[5]

I have never made any other colors. Poor farmers like me make red with iron oxide, but fancy painters use cinnabar, a red metal found in the ore of mercury. Blue is made from azurite, a copper ore or from the mineral lapis lazuli which is very expensive. The mineral malachite is used for making green.[6] Of course if you have blue and yellow you make your own green."

"How do you make yellow?" Sadie asked.

"I read in one of Uncle Benjamin's books that yellow is made with red lead and tin and baked in a furnace. I have no idea how they do it. Of course azurite, lapis lazuli and malachite are not local minerals."

Sadie looked disappointed. "How will we make our paints?"

"Perhaps your mother can write to your Peabody relatives in Boston to inquire about purchasing pigments. I can teach you how to add the linseed oil."

"That could take forever," she glumly responded.

"What do you think artists paint on?" Ethan asked.

"Paper?"

"You can write and draw on paper, but you cannot paint on paper. Artists use wood panels, canvas or metal plates.[7] I have old, dried wood panels in my workshop you can use. You should never use green wood, because it will shrink."

"We have an attic filled with canvas," Grace smiled at her daughter. "You know my father was a ship builder. When I moved to Fryeburg from Boston, the servants carefully wrapped each piece of furniture in canvas before packing it into a wooden crate stuffed with straw.

The straw and wood are long gone but your grandmother stored the canvas in the attic. Papa can cut it into the sizes you want."

"Before you paint, you must prepare the wood or canvas. You cannot paint directly on the wood, because the wood will absorb some of the paint. You must first coat it with rabbit glue. Also you must prepare the canvas by stretching it and coating it with rabbit glue.[8] This is a skill unto itself. You should practice this before you even begin to paint.

Not all pigments are made from minerals; some are made from plants mixed with egg whites. I can give you the recipes and you can begin experimenting with colors today."

"We have plenty of eggs!" Sadie's eyes lit up.

"For red, boil the red roots of the madder plant until the water turns red. Combine some of the red water with the egg whites. Place dried, crushed saffron flowers into a small cloth bag in a dish of egg whites. The yellow color will seep out of the bag making a thin yellow paint. Crush fresh parsley with a mortar and pestle until a deep green juice comes out. Then mix the juice with egg whites. Be sure to beat the egg whites in a bowl until it becomes foamy.[9]

"What about red and blue?"

"When your pigments arrive, you can mix the red and blue pigments with the egg whites."

"Do you mean mix them together?"

"No. I mean separately. If you mix them together you will make purple. If you add white to purple you will make lavender."

"I can make my own colors!"

Grace added, "You make orange by mixing yellow and red. Adding white paint will make your colors lighter; adding black paint will make them darker."

Sadie then knew she wanted to spend the rest of her life making colors.

It took Ethan several years to complete the two-storied "Benjamin Miller House". The basement and the granite foundation was a feat in itself. In the cellar stood a great stone archway upon which stood a huge chimney with many fireplaces.

Ethan and Benjamin had designed and redesigned the impressive front façade. The front door stood upon three semi-circular, granite steps, flanked by two long windows. A semi-circular window graced the top of the door. All of this was framed by two wooden columns. Directly above was the second story window which was curved on the top and flanked by two, long, narrow windows.[10]

As one entered the foyer Benjamin's expansive office was to the right. This room which took the entire half of the first floor served as his study, office and conference room. Interior walls were lined with book cases. The family's dining room/sitting room was located to the left of the foyer and in front of the kitchen, hearth and pantry. Both a large circular staircase in the foyer and a smaller set of stairs from the kitchen led to several spacious bedrooms on the second floor. Numerous windows let in plenty of natural light.

Benjamin and Hannah held opposite opinions when it came to their furniture. Hannah preferred utilitarian furniture with simple lines and light colored stains. Benjamin appreciated fine wood working and wanted intricately carved tables and chairs. Ethan found a compromise by declaring the kitchen and bedrooms to be Hannah's domain and she would select the furniture. Benjamin's office and the dining room would be used for the family as well as his clients therefore he would select the furniture. This solution pleased everyone and Ethan was finally able to get to work "in peace".

In the summer of 1800 the family and several students of Fryeburg Academy loaded wagons filled with furniture, books, linens, cooking utensils, dishes, bedding and children for the short half mile trip down the road from Riverview Farm to the Preceptor's House.

Benjamin directed the placement of furniture in his rooms. No one was allowed to open his trunks of books or place them on the built- in book cases. The Chippendale desk imported from London before the war, was a wedding gift from Grace and Micah. Ethan and Benjamin carefully placed it by the front window. A sitting area consisting of two wing backed chairs and an end table was arranged in front of the Franklin stove. A smaller writing desk and deacon's bench was placed in the back corner by the window. A large oval table in the center of the room would serve as a conference table. As a house warming gift, Ethan had intricately carved a black walnut plaque which read:

> *What doth the LORD require of thee,*
> *But to do justly,*
> *And to love mercy*
> *And to walk humbly with thy God.*
> *Micah 6:8*

A magnificent, black walnut, drop leaf table sat in the middle of the dining room with four matching chairs upholstered with leather cushions. Additional chairs were lined against the wall. A black walnut side board sat between the two front windows. The large looking glass was strategically placed above the side board and directly across from the fireplace, to reflect the firelight. A black leather settee sat against the interior wall. With all the seats and with the table leaves pulled out, this room could comfortably accommodate sixteen people.

Hannah had requested that Ethan build her a smaller version of the Liberty Table of white pine and one large, matching cupboard for her kitchen. Sarah, Grace and Hannah efficiently stocked the kitchen and pantry with crockery, pans, bowls, simple dishes and cooking utensils as Libby and Sade watched the younger children in the yard.

Upstairs, each child had the luxury of their own bed and cabinet in their own rooms with colorful hooked rugs scattered on the floor. Sarah had woven a simple, white, wool coverlet for the four poster bed and matching white bed curtains and canopy. One large oak wardrobe, two bureaus and a lady's dressing table completed the room.

"Benjamin and I would love to have the family over for Sunday dinner next week," Hannah invited flushed with excitement. "The following Friday evening we are having a social for Reverend and Mrs. Fessenden and other trustees and their wives. Twice a month we will have a tea for students and their parents."

"That is very ambitions," Grace admired.

"A wise woman once told me, a wife needs to support her husband in his career," she smiled.

"I would love to help you with the arrangements," Grace, who enjoyed entertaining, eagerly offered.

"I will watch the children," Sarah, who relished her role as grandmother, volunteered.

"I was counting on that," Hannah smiled.

Hannah took great pride in being the mistress of her own home and her reputation for hospitality was spreading throughout Fryeburg. Benjamin's students were always welcomed with a smile and a glass of cider. Students needing tutoring in Greek and Latin spent Saturday mornings around the conference table with textbooks in one hand and cornbread in the other. However it was the evenings after putting the children to bed and sitting quietly by the Franklin stove with Benjamin that were her favorite moments. "Benjamin, I have discovered it is more difficult for one mother to watch two children than for two mothers to watch five."

"Why not invite Grace and the children over to tea some afternoons," her husband suggested. "I am certain Jacob and Alden would enjoy their time together and my mother may appreciate the quiet."

Other evenings she would embroider, sew or hook another rug while Benjamin excitedly discussed the upcoming reelection of President John Adams or the most recent letter to the Millers from First Lady, Abigail Adams. Sometimes she would read while her husband corrected Latin tests or Greek translations.

One blustery October evening a pounding on the back door startled them.

"Ethan, where is your coat? What is wrong?" Hannah asked in concern as she led her brother-in-law to a seat by the hearth.

"Do I need to get Dr. Emery? Is someone ill?" Benjamin asked as he headed for his cloak.

"I asked Mr. Colby for Nancy's hand in marriage and she turned me down. She has made her promise to Jonathan Knowles," he shook his head in disbelief.[11]

"Any woman would be honored to marry someone like you!" Hannah exclaimed with indignation.

Ethan pulled out a rumpled letter from his back pocket and handed it to Benjamin. "Do you remember Daniel Merrill, the master carpenter from Ireland who built our house addition? He has asked me to become his business partner and buy a cabinetmaker's shop with him. It is an opportunity of a lifetime. I was not going to accept the offer if I married Nancy. Now I must. If I remain in Fryeburg I will always be a part time farmer and a second rate carpenter."

"Well congratulations," Benjamin slapped his brother on the back. "Boston is not so far away."

"I am not moving to Boston. I am moving to Williamsburg."

"To Virginia?" Hannah gasped.

"Benjamin, I know what you are going to say. I should not go."

"On the contrary, dear brother, I believe this is Providential."

The rest of the Millers greeted the news of Ethan's departure with shock and grief. "Uncle Ethan, would you deprive me of an uncle's love for the rest of my life?" Libby dramatically asked.

"You still have Uncle Benjamin," Ethan pointed out.

"You know as well as I that Uncle Benjamin is no fun and he does not spoil me!"

"Ethan, I understand that you are upset. Please do not make a rash decision that all of us will regret," Micah reasoned.

"When Benjamin left fourteen years ago, no one attempted to stop him," Ethan countered.

"We did not need Benjamin. But we need you!"

Grace interjected, "I have grown to love you as a brother."

"You are more than a brother to me," Micah continued, "You are my best friend."

James intervened, for Sarah was too stricken to speak, "Ethan, you are an invaluable member of this family and none of us want you to leave. However, if the Lord is leading you on this venture it is unfair for us to try to stop you. Your mother and I left our home, our church and her family when we moved to Fryeburg in 1765. William Bradford left his family back in England when he boarded the Mayflower in 1620. The Israelites left Egypt for the Promised Land. Abraham left his father's house in the city of Ur to follow the Lord. I will not quarrel that sometimes the Lord requires us to leave our homes to follow Him." The matter was settled.

Sadie ran upstairs to her bedroom and sobbed.

Ethan spent the next two weeks carefully wrapping and packing his tools in two large wooden chests. Sarah washed, mended and packed his clothing in one of the oak chests which Grace had brought with her when she arrived in March of 1781. The Fryes, the Walkers, the Osgoods with Limbo, the Ames, Reverend and Mrs. Fessenden, Mr. and Mrs. Ephraim Weston all stopped by to wish him well and to say their good byes.

"Lt. Osgood, I regret that I will be unable to build your addition to the Oxford House. I am sure it will be a grand inn and respite for weary travelers."

"Mr. Weston, it is good to have neighbors across the street."

"I have appreciated your help in finishing up the barn. We all will miss you, Ethan. I understand not everyone was cut out to be a farmer. We wish you the best of luck with your new business."

"Sadie, I wrote down all the recipes for your paints. You have a good supply of cut and framed canvas and your Papa can make more. I expect that you will send me beautiful paintings of Riverview Farm and Fryeburg."

"I expect that you will write us often," she replied.

Early one November morning, Micah loaded the wagon with Ethan's three trunks and six crates of furniture ready to take his brother to Portland to board a ship. At Ethan's request and to Sadie's delight, Sadie boarded the wagon sitting snuggled between her father and uncle.

"James, you have a letter from Ethan," Postmaster Moses Ames announced many days later as he delivered the letter directly to the Liberty Table by the hearth. The family eagerly gathered around as James began to read.

November 1800
Boston,
Massachusetts

Dear Family,

This Fryeburg farm boy was ever so grateful to arrive in Boston on solid ground! I do not know how Grace's father managed to spend half his life out to sea. Our cousin Nathaniel Bradford met me at the wharf and brought me to his home for a few days and showed me around the city. Boston is a busy, noisy, crowded place.

Mr. and Mrs. Thomas Peabody were kind enough to invite me to tea. They were fascinated by the story of how we built our addition on the house back in 1781and wanted to hear about my cabinetmaking businesses. When they learned I was bringing some unsold furniture with me to Virginia, they asked to see my black walnut armoire. They paid a very handsome price for it! They claimed someday their Miller armoire will be as valuable as their Chippendale.

I have never seen such an elegant home in my life – that is until I walked past John Hancock's mansion. Grace, it must have been quite a shock moving from Boston to our humble little farm house.

Tomorrow, Nathaniel is taking me to Lexington to meet Uncle Jacob and the rest of the family. Nathaniel greatly resembles Benjamin and he was surprised to discover that I "looked like a Viking". I told him I have never seen a Viking but I do strongly resemble my father.

First thing Wednesday morning I board another ship and start for Washington D.C. then on to Williamsburg.

I hope everyone is well.

Yours truly,

Ethan

After reading the letter out loud, James refolded the letter and handed it to Libby, "Please run this up to Uncle Benjamin. I am sure he will be most eager to read it."

Three weeks later a grinning Moses Ames handed Sarah two letters. "Madam, it appears you have received a letter from the First Lady and your third son." Sarah ripped open Ethan's letter first.

> *Washington, D.C.*
> *December 1800*

Dear Mother,

I had the honor of meeting Mrs. Abigail Adams. She treated me like her long-lost son and wanted to hear everything about the family. I felt very much at ease with her - perhaps because she is so much like you.

I told her I had a gift for the President from the Miller family and delivered my cherry desk. Well, President Adams appeared and proclaimed it was a "fine, New England desk" and he would set it up in his office. He was very proper and polite but I liked Mrs. Adams much better.

I told Mrs. Adams how sorry we were that Mr. Adams lost the election to Thomas Jefferson. Benjamin always said there is no other man more qualified or dedicated to be our President.

She seemed pleased with those sentiments. However she is quite content to return to their home in Quincy and to enjoy a quiet life. She hopes Mother will come to visit her there.

The federal city and the President's mansion were quite a disappointment. I would not call it a city at all. It is more like a collection of unfinished buildings surrounded by wilderness and swamps. I dare say our own Riverview Farm is far more suitable for the President of our new Republic than what President and Mrs. Adams is currently residing. I do not wonder that Mrs. Adams is eager to return to her domicile.

I found the sight of poorly treated slaves laboring to build our government buildings to be a mockery of liberty.

Your loving son,
Ethan

December 1800
Washington, D.C.

My Dearest Sarah,

I spent the most delightful afternoon with your son, Ethan. He looks just like his father. I know while you must be proud of his abilities and wish him success with his new enterprise I understand a mother's grief in watching her beloved child leave home.

Ethan had me laughing at all the stories he had about the family and Grace. It was providential that Grace was sent to live with you. I can imagine her now a lovely grown woman, a wife and mother and homemaker. It feels like it was only yesterday that Elizabeth and I were having tea while Grace, Nabby and John Quincy were playing in the nursery.

Ethan is a talented young man and I am confident that his new business will prosper. John was most appreciative of Ethan's generous gift. We both shall cherish it for years to come.

Now that I have met Ethan, I wish to meet the rest of your family. Once we are settled back home in Braintree, you must come to visit. Thirty-five years of separation is much too long!

Fondly,
Abigail

Although Sarah Miller was a humble woman she did not object to Grace and Hannah discussing with the ladies after church Ethan's visit with the President and First Lady of the United States. If Mrs. Colby just happened to overhear that conversation, all the better!

X

Williamsburg

January, 1801
Williamsburg, Virginia

Dear Family,

I do not know where to begin. I believe I will like this town. It is not dirty and crowded like Boston; it is not unfinished and incomplete like Washington; it is not quiet and isolated like Fryeburg. The houses are planted neatly and orderly like our apple trees in the orchard. The homes are tidy and well kept. I can walk from the boarding house to my shop as well to all the shops, taverns and to church.

The Merrills welcomed me with open arms and invited me to live with them. Although I enjoyed being Uncle Ethan to their six children, after two weeks I decided I would rent a room at a local boarding house. Mother, I assure you that you would approve of my lodgings for they are clean and comfortable with a view of their small back yard. However, I find the cooking wanting, and I fear that I will starve.

I think of my Miller ladies everyday as I walk past a dress maker's shop on my way to work. Of course I have no reason to go in, but the dresses and hats displayed in the window are very pretty.

I have not had the opportunity to meet many people yet. I have been spending every waking hour moving into the shop and settling into work.

The shop is more than I had hoped for! It is large with plenty of windows to let in the light. The first room serves as a showroom where we display our furniture. The second room is quite spacious with two work benches and plenty of room for any future apprentices. Now I understand how Benjamin felt when he unpacked his books and organized them on his book shelves! I spent two whole days just organizing and reorganizing my tools.

Daniel's work area is even larger than mine. There is also storage space on the second floor.

It grows late and my candle is burning down. I wanted to write you all a brief note to let you know that I have arrived safely and I am getting settled.

I miss you all,

Ethan

P.S. Sadie, I found your painting of the sheep grazing by the Saco in the bottom on my trunk. I have hung it in my room above my small writing table. When I feel homesick, I look at it and I feel like I am home again.

March, 1801
Williamsburg, Virginia

Dear Family,

I am pleased to say business is going well. I have sold my two remaining desks after Daniel boasted that President Adams invited me to tea and one of my desks served him while he was President. Some of the ladies are impressed that Mother and Mrs. Adams are close friends. However, everyone in town – in the state of Virginia for that matter - talks of nothing but Jefferson's inauguration. They are of the opinion that only gentlemen from Virginia are qualified to be President!

Daniel insisted that I attend a social in the home of a very prominent citizen in order to make my acquaintance with potential customers with "discriminating tastes". I felt like a crow in a barnyard of swans! They do all these fancy dances. Although several brazen young ladies invited me to dance, I politely declined. (Mother would not approve of their immodest dress.) "I guess Puritans do not dance," they declared with distain.

Socializing with the men did not go much better, for all they talked about were politics and the price of tobacco. I smiled and listened politely. They were all dressed up in velvets and silks. Not one of them had any calluses on their hands. These dandies would be laughed out of the town of Fryeburg.

A Mrs. Edwards, the owner of the dressmaker shop, came to my rescue when she admired the quality of the wool of my waistcoat. I told her all about our sheep, about Mother's spinning and weaving and about the day Grace came to live with us. I had never seen so many petticoats in my life.

Then I spent the rest of the evening talking about how Benjamin left for Harvard and became an attorney. Then I rambled about Micah and Grace's wedding day and all my "Uncle Ethan" stories of Libby and Sadie. I told her how Benjamin brought Hannah to Fryeburg from Philadelphia and they got married. I told them about the day Alden and Benjamin were born.

She asked why a man who loved children so much was not married and had his own family. Naturally I told her how Nancy Colby refused my proposal in order to marry Jonathan Knowles.

She said Fryeburg's loss is Williamsburg's gain. She told me she has a six-year-old daughter named Margaret who "helps" her with the customers. Maggie sounds very much like Libby.

The evening was not a total loss. The food was very good and plentiful, although it upset me to see slaves serving the food. I told Mrs. Edwards that back in Fryeburg the women took pride in cooking and serving their own food. Two older gentlemen promised to stop by the shop on Monday morning to discuss furniture.

I miss you all,
Ethan

May 1801
Williamsburg, Virginia

Dear Family,

Sadie, thank you for your letters and I beg your forgiveness for allowing two whole months to pass without writing. I am pleased to report that we have so many orders for furniture that we have hired two apprentices. Several of the homes have floor coverings of painted

149

canvas. Many are simply geometric designs but some have flowers or scenes. I am sure you could paint some canvas floor coverings just as nice as I have seen here. I would not be surprised if Uncle Benjamin bought one for his dining room.

Jacob, Mrs. Edwards helped me select this fabric for your grandmother to make you a waistcoat. As you know I was the youngest boy who always wore his brothers' hand-me-downs just as you wear Alden's hand-me-downs. I thought you might want a waistcoat made especially for you.

I did not forget "my girls". The ribbons are for Libby, Sadie and Abigail.

Father and Micah, have you begun to plant or is there still a danger of frost? You would be amazed at the long growing season down here. People have just begun to pick from their kitchen gardens. Mother, I am delighted that you, Grace and Hannah will be visiting with Mrs. Adams next month. However, I do not feel it is safe for you ladies to travel unescorted. Since Benjamin is done with school for the summer, I think it would be more appropriate that he escort you.

Benjamin, the enclosed quill is for you. Please stop terrorizing the geese.

Always,
Ethan

P.S. I have recently learned that Mrs. Edwards is a widow.

August, 1801
Williamsburg, Virginia

Dear Benjamin,

I see no need for you to be angry with me just because I told President Adams that when you were a boy you sat at the Chippendale desk and pretended to be an attorney like him and you were envious of John Quincy's opportunities. You were only fourteen years old then. You are much too concerned about other people's opinions of you. As Hannah would say, "that is a vanity!" I do hope you did not brood about it and ruin the visit for everyone else.

Yesterday I witnessed my first slave auction. I crossed the street to avoid the crowd but I could not look away. They sold a little boy, not older than ten or twelve, right out of his mother's arms. I will never forget her screams and cries.

I was so upset that I ran into Olivia's dress shop and told her that I do not belong here. I do not dance, or smoke tobacco, or waste my time playing cards. I do not like their politics.

She told me that the Lord sent me here for a greater purpose than to run away from a failed romance. I should pray and seek His will.

I asked her how she could bear to live her life in freedom and see so many slaves doing jobs that white people should do for themselves. She told me that until the day women enjoy the same freedoms as men, I should not be accusing her of living her life in "freedom". "Does not the North have slaves? Has not your friend Limbo been bought and sold? Is he free to leave or marry? Are there not ship builders up north who make a fine profit

151

building slave ships? Are not the plantation owners some of your best customers? Hypocrisy does not become you, Mr. Miller. Good day, Sir. We both have work to do."

Do all women act like Grace? What makes me so angry is that Olivia is right.

I am hungry, hot, tired and cross. Give my love to the family. I will write them when I am in better spirits.

Your Brother,
Ethan

October 1801
Williamsburg, Virginia

Dear Father,

Thank you for your response to my last letter. I suppose a son is never too old to need his father's wisdom. You are right. I should not ask myself will Olivia make a good wife for me. I should ask will I make a good husband for her. I believe the answer is yes to both questions.

Olivia is talented and determined like Grace; wise and dignified like Hannah and Godly and concerned for others like Mother. She challenges me to think more deeply. I fear until I left Fryeburg I had led a sheltered life. I wished I had listened more closely to Benjamin's never- ending discussions around the Liberty Table and read some of his books.

When Olivia's husband died, his property went to his younger brother - leaving Olivia and two-year old Maggie destitute. She returned home to live with her parents. Her father set up the dressmaking business and her mother cared for Maggie. Although the business has grown very prosperous, it is still her father's business.

I could build us our own home and buy the dress shop from her father and give it to her. I am not content to spend the rest of my life being Uncle Ethan. I want to be a Papa with my own children. I would love Maggie as my own. I understand Olivia's excitement in making a garment when she finds just the right fabric. I feel the same way when I get my hands on some cherry wood or black walnut. More importantly than providing her with a home and business, I would give her my love and fidelity.

I am glad to learn that you as a poor pastor were also terrified to ask the esteemed Mr. Bradford for his youngest daughter's hand in marriage. I will not procrastinate like I did the last time. I am now an established business man ready for the responsibilities of a family.

Your Loving Son,
Ethan

November, 1801
Williamsburg, Virginia

Dear Benjamin,

I guess by now the family has received my letter stating that Olivia and I will be married in her parents' home on New Year's Day. It will be a small gathering of just her family and the Merrills. That is fine with me!

I have purchased a small home on the outskirts of town which has enough land for me to build a large addition as the family grows. Olivia's father has generously offered to give her the dress shop as a wedding gift. We thanked him and told him I would have my attorney (that is you) draw up the papers.

Also Maggie wants to "marry" me as well. Olivia says Maggie does not remember her father and she has no contact with the Edwards side of the family. Could I adopt her and then all of us would be Millers?

Were you this nervous before your wedding? I wish all of you could be at the wedding!

Your Brother,
Ethan

April, 1802
Williamsburg, Virginia

Dear Family,

Please do not scold me for not writing sooner. I have been very busy! Right now I am timber framing our summer kitchen. I can hear Libby asking what is wrong with the kitchen we have. Well, summers are insufferably hot and heating up the house from May to October to cook is simply intolerable. Many families have a small outbuilding behind the house that serves as a second kitchen, a laundry and an extra pantry. Olivia laughs that her Yankee will one day acclimate to the weather.

Olivia and I cannot thank you enough for your generosity! The trunk you sent us arrived yesterday. I recognized it as one of Grace's old trunks she brought with her from Boston and feared it would be filled with old petticoats. Benjamin, I thank you for the books. I will read Calvin's Institutes first. Olivia wisely insists that the Lord's Day be devoted to reading and meditation after communal worship. Jacob, did you make those baskets by yourself? You are very talented and I greatly appreciate having three baskets without ribbons and bows!

I will let Olivia convey her thanks.

Dear Millers,

Thank you for your kind words and welcoming me into the family. I promised Ethan that someday we will take a trip up to Fryeburg and visit. Grace, I can never thank you enough for the wedding gift of your mother's silver candlesticks made by Paul Revere! Mother Miller, I have never seen such a beautiful hooked rug. Libby, I thank you for the skeins of yarn. Did you spin the yarn yourself on your grandmother's spinning wheel? Although your uncle claims that the Virginian winters are not cold, I will knit scarves and mittens for Maggie and myself.

Sadie, Uncle Ethan had tears in his eyes when he unpacked your painting of Riverview Farm. I now truly understand why he gets homesick. He promptly hung it over the mantle and declared that now this house is a home.

Our love to you all,
Olivia, Ethan and Maggie.

November, 1802
Williamsburg, Virginia

Dear Benjamin,

I was surprised to hear from Micah's letter than you are no longer teaching at Fryeburg Academy. Fryeburg and the surrounding towns must be rapidly growing if you have more work than you can handle in your law practice. He told me that Seth Spring has opened a new store and there is a tailor in town. Is that where you buy "your fancy lawyer clothes"? Those are Micah's words and not mine.

Last week I received my first letter from Limbo telling me all about the arrival of Daniel Webster, the new preceptor. He is such a good story teller I could imagine every detail:

Mrs. Osgood told me to ready the nicest bedroom on the second floor that overlooks the main street for we had a guest staying with us for the whole school year. It just did not feel right that Mr. Benjamin was not teaching no more. Well a wagon pulled up in front and I welcomed him to the Oxford House, introduced myself to young Mr. Webster, then grabbed his trunk and carried it upstairs.

"I told him I remember Mr. Benjamin's first day of teaching. He was all dressed up like he was going to one of his fancy court rooms back in Philadelphia. I told him not to be nervous because he was a fine teacher. He taught Old Limbo to read and write. It is a fine thing to be a teacher. If I could be anything in the world, I would be a teacher and teach anybody who could not go to school.

"Mr. Benjamin Miller, the preceptor taught you to read?"

"Sure did, sir, when he was just a boy. He was the smartest young boy I ever knew. He was always getting into trouble for reading and not doing his farm chores, though. Now that school is almost busting at the seams. Mr. Benjamin had his father Elder Miller teaching those farm boys those fancy languages back at Riverview Farm. Mr. Benjamin teaches awfully fast and some of those boys had a hard time keeping up. So Mr. Miller gave some of those boys some extra help. Not that I blame them. Have you seen those fancy Greek letters? You have to learn a new alphabet and everything. It seems like a lot of work just to get yourself into Harvard. Did you go to Harvard, too?"

"No, Limbo, after I graduated from Philips Exeter I went to Dartmouth College in New Hampshire."

"I never heard of it. Did you always want to be a teacher?"

"No. I want to be a lawyer but I am teaching to earn some money to put my older brother, Ezekiel through college. I need to make as much money as I can."

"Lt. Osgood needs help writing deeds and Mr. Benjamin has more lawyer work than he knows what to do with. I bet you could make some extra money helping them."

"Limbo, you have been a fountain of knowledge. Could you introduce me to the esteemed Attorney Miller?"

"He lives in that fancy white house on the corner. I can bring you by after supper."

"Is there anything else I should know, Limbo?"

"Yes, be sure you are in time for meals. Aunt Nabby does not take kindly to people late for supper."

"Is Aunt Nabby the cook?"

"Everyone calls Mrs. Osgood Aunt Nabby and she runs the Oxford House. If you need anything, you let me know. Just make sure you are not late for your meals."

Please tell Limbo that I look forward to his next letter.

My big news is that Olivia is with child. I should be a Papa sometime around Christmas. I have built a cradle and she has made some clothes. Maggie is knitting baby blankets.

Give my love to all.

Ethan

February, 1803
Williamsburg, Virginia

Dear Family,

I am pleased to announce that Matthew James Miller was born on December 24, 1802. He was larger than Jacob but smaller than Alden.

Olivia says I am a natural handling the baby. I told her that I had much practice with my nieces and nephews!

Sadie, I am sending you some pigment of a new color called Prussian Blue. When I saw some blue wainscoting at a client's home, I inquired around town how I could find some pigment.

I will write again, soon.

Ethan

September, 1803
Williamsburg, Virginia

Dear Family,

I was sorry to hear that young Mr. Webster has left town to return to his legal apprenticeship in New Hampshire. I can imagine Benjamin enjoyed discussing politics with a fellow federalist and will miss him. Do he and Micah still argue all the time?

The summer kitchen has been finally completed. The shop is busy as ever and I have hired another apprentice who is also helping me with a much needed addition to the house now that we are expecting another child. Olivia has hired an older woman and experienced seamstress to help run the shop.

Could it be possible that our Libby is now seventeen years old? Mother says that she looks very much like

Grace and young men are already coming around wanting to court her.

Father says Sadie's paintings are works of art. Perhaps if you ship some to me, I will make some frames and Olivia could sell them in her shop for Sadie.

Did Jacob forget his Uncle Ethan? Alden and Abigail write to me and tell me all about the village school and life on the farm but I never hear from him.

Matthew is crying for his Papa and I promised Maggie I would read her a story before bedtime.

Olivia sends her love.

Faithfully,

Ethan

March, 1804

Williamsburg, Virginia

Dear Family,

Please forgive me for not writing sooner. Matthew James Miller now has a new brother, Mark Bradford Miller. I now have two sons to help me in the shop!

The addition to the house is almost complete. Olivia's father has been helping with it and Olivia's mother watches Matthew, who is a handful, while Olivia tends to Mark. I remember how mother spent her time with Libby and Sadie when they were young. I now understand why Benjamin wanted to move back to Fryeburg.

Mother, thank you for writing so faithfully. Olivia and I cherish your letters.

Fondly,

Ethan, Olivia, Maggie, Matthew and Mark

April, 1804
Williamsburg, Virginia

Dear Benjamin,

I cannot speak of the evil I witnessed last week. Slavery is like a piece of mold on a loaf of cornbread. If it is not cut out, it will spoil the whole loaf.

What can one man do? I try to be an example. I do not own slaves; I pay my apprentices fairly and treat them with respect. I built my house additions myself to show others that there is honor and dignity in working with my hands.

Yet, I know that I am not blameless. Slavery feeds my children and makes my business successful. My biggest customers are the wealthy plantation owners. Even my other customers, who buy smaller pieces, pay me with the money they earned from providing their services to the plantation owners. It is not only the very wealthy who have slaves. Several families right here in town have them as well.

What can I do? Even if I packed up the family and started over in Fryeburg, nothing would change here.

I fear that God will judge me for doing nothing.
Ethan

XI

Spilt Ink

Ten-year-old Jacob stared out the window of his father's office watching the robin making its nest. Life was so unfair. It was bad enough to be imprisoned five days a week at the village school but now his father demanded that Jacob spend this beautiful Saturday morning in May indoors practicing his penmanship.

He sighed and wondered if Uncle Micah's two mares were going to foal today. He wondered how many acres the oxen could plough today. There had not been a frost in two weeks. Would it be safe to plant crops this soon? Uncle Micah sheared the sheep three days ago, and Jacob promised Sadie he would help her wash the fleece and lay it out in the sun to dry.

Why did he have to go to school when there were so many more important things he could be doing? His classmates called him "Jacob the Dreamer". His teacher sent letters home to his father complaining about his impertinent behavior and how he needs to try harder.

He rarely saw his father, who spent every waking hour cloistered in his study six days and six nights a week.

Many evenings he did not even appear to eat supper with the family. It felt like the only time his father spoke to him, it was to criticize. "Why can you not be more like your sister?" his father asked in exasperation on more than one occasion. Abigail had the best penmanship in the school and she read five grade levels above him.

Being Alden's cousin only made the situation intolerable. Tall, strong, and handsome like his father, Alden was the teacher's favorite and the smartest boy in the school.

Why could they not understand how hard he was trying to decipher these symbols into meaning? He dipped his quill into the ink pot. With all of his concentration he tried to copy the letter j to write his name. A blob of ink slowly dripped down the page.

"Jacob! Watch what you are doing!" his father reprimanded.

Startled, he moved suddenly and knocked over the ink pot. He watched the ink slowly spread across the Chippendale desk. "You fool! Look what you have done!" Benjamin's back hand to his son's face sent him sprawling over the chair onto the floor. "Can you do nothing right?"

Hannah came running into her husband's office. "You are his father! You are not his master!" she screamed at Benjamin.

"I hate you! I wish Uncle Micah was my father and not you!" Jacob sobbed and ran from the house toward his grandparents' farm.

"You are a selfish, arrogant man!" Hannah threw his copy of Samuel's Rutherford's *Lex Rex* across the room before running after Jacob.

"Papa, may I help you clean the stain?" Abigail asked timidly with a rag in her hand.

"Leave it be!" he snapped as he picked up important papers and neatly stacked them on a book shelf. He had three clients scheduled for the afternoon. "Just look at this mess," he muttered."

"Uncle Ethan can make you a new desk," Abigail offered.

"This desk is irreplaceable! Now leave it be!" he yelled and his daughter quietly left the room.

It was getting dark when Benjamin lit the candle on his desk. His family should have been home hours ago he thought gloomily. He jumped up and ran to the back door at the sound of his brother's wagon stopping. To his disappointment, his father arrived alone.

"Shall we talk in your office?" James asked solemnly as he entered the back door. After being seated, James simply stated, "I believe it is in Jacob's best interest if he came to live with me."

"What? What do you mean it is in his best interest? Why?"

"What does the sixth chapter of Ephesians, verse 4 say?" James asked quietly.

"Children, obey your parents in the Lord: for this is right."

"No. That is the third verse. Verse 4 says, 'And, ye fathers, provoke not your children to wrath: but bring them up in the nurture and admonition of the Lord'. Benjamin, you are breaking Jacob's spirit. You are so intent upon his faults that you are blind to his many talents. You are so consumed with your law practice that you have neglected to train and instruct him in the ways of the Lord. You have taught many young men in town, yet your own son is failing in school. My question is who is the failure? Is it Jacob or is it you?"

Benjamin sat there in stunned silence for several minutes before speaking. "I am guilty as charged, sir. Let me take you home and I will apologize to my son."

"Apologizing is a good first step. Repentance requires more than words; it requires a change in actions, a change of attitude and a change of heart. Do not apologize to your family until you are ready to change. Anything less is simply hypocrisy." With those words, James stood up and left.

Benjamin took a deep breath and closed his eyes. His father called him a hypocrite. Hannah called him arrogant and Jacob hated him. He was proud that he could read the Scriptures in Hebrew and Greek, yet he no longer lived the Scriptures. He taught others all about God, yet he no longer knew Him. He was proud of his scholarship, his position as preceptor and of attorney. He was more concerned about his reputation than his son's struggles.

Pride can blind a man to the truth. Now he painfully saw that it was he and not Jacob who was the failure.

Benjamin found Jacob in the barn with Micah and Alden doing evening chores.

"Jacob, I have come to ask for your forgiveness for I have made many mistakes. I fear that my mistakes have hurt you deeply."

"You did?"

"Yes, my first mistake was not hiring an assistant when Mr. Webster left. I was foolish to assume I could run this practice by myself. First thing Monday morning I will make some inquiries in hiring another attorney. I have neglected my parental responsibilities.

I am told that I am a very good teacher. This summer the two of us will spend evenings together so I may tutor you. I was wrong to criticize you when I refused to teach you myself.

Farming is a noble endeavor and I failed to recognize your talents in that area. I see now that you can be a great help to your grandfather and uncle this summer. When school resumes in the fall you may spend each afternoon and all day Saturday on the farm. I dare say there are several projects at home which need to be done which I will need your help.

Your grandfather feels it is in your best interest that you live with him. I have a proposal. I ask that you return home with me to see if I am able to make right my many wrongs. If I have failed to do so by the time school resumes in the autumn, you may choose to stay here at the farm. I simply ask that you give me the opportunity to make things up to you."

"It takes a big man to admit his mistakes," Jacob stated with all the wisdom of a ten-year-old. "We are all sinners. If we want people to forgive us, then we must be willing to forgive others."

"Did Reverend Fessenden teach you that?"

"No, sir. You did."

"Your grandfather taught me. Now I must apologize to your mother."

"Did her father teach her to forgive too?"

"I pray so, Jacob. I pray so."

The wagon dropped Joshua Caleb Pierce at the front door of the Oxford House. Limbo opened the door and welcomed his guest, "Mr. Pierce, you do not look like a lawyer. You look like a farmer!"

"My good man, that is an astute observation," Joshua smiled easily. "You see I was born and raised on a farm. My mother made me two good suits for Sundays and lawyer work and she made me promise to pack them carefully in my trunk so not to get them dusty and dirty on the journey. I promise you, sir, once I am unpacked and washed up I shall look like a lawyer. At the very least, I shall look like a farmer trying to look like a lawyer. I just graduated from Dartmouth four days ago and this is my first job interview."

"Mr. Pierce, let me carry this trunk to your room," Limbo offered. On the fifth step, the leather handle broke resulting in the trunk falling down the stairs spilling its contents into the parlor.

"Limbo, please be more careful!" Abigail Osgood admonished as she hurried over.

"It is not Limbo's fault, Madam. This old trunk belonged to my grandfather when he left England for Boston before the war. This leather strap was frayed and should have been replaced years ago. My father lost the key years ago so I could not lock it," he explained as he picked up and folded his clothing and placed them back into his trunk. "Sir, if you would be so kind as to hold one end while I take the other, I believe the two of us could carry this up to my room without further mishap.

Madam, if you could kindly point out the way to Mr. Miller's office, I have a two o'clock interview."

The young man failed to realize that the gentleman and young boy sitting so quietly in the corner were observing it all. Joshua Pierce had just passed his first job interview.

Late the next afternoon, Benjamin asked Jacob, "Before supper will you please run to the farm and ask Uncle Micah if I may borrow his oxen tomorrow? I think the two of us should plant a small herb and kitchen garden in the back yard.

"Really? You and I are going to plant a garden?"

"Yes, I believe we will. Now run along."

Twenty minutes later Jacob returned looking uncertain. "Well? What did your Uncle Micah say?"

"Umm. Umm…" he stuttered nervously.

"Let me guess. He said, 'Your father does not know which end of an ox to feed. Tell him he may not borrow my oxen, but I will be there first thing tomorrow morning and plough it myself!'"

Jacob laughed out loud. "How did you know?"

Benjamin smiled and tapped his right temple with his fore finger. "He may be bigger, stronger and better looking, but I will always be smarter. Never tell him I said that."

"I promise," he stated solemnly as he stifled a giggle. "I promise."

Jacob, Benjamin and Joshua surveyed the newly ploughed patch in the backyard. "Mr. Pierce, would you be kind enough to take my two o'clock appointment? Jacob and I are going to plant Mrs. Miller a small garden. If you need me, I will be right here."

"Yes, sir!" Joshua was thrilled to think that he would begin to see clients on his second day of work. "May I suggest that you plant some flowers as well?"

"That is an excellent suggestion. I am sure Mrs. Miller would be delighted to have flowers."

"I am sure she will. However, I was thinking the flowers would attract bees."

"Bees?"

"Yes, sir. The flowers will attract the bees which will help pollinate the garden. Sir, if you need me, I will be in your office."

"Father, oregano grows like a weed. We should be certain to leave plenty of room before we plant the thyme or they will crowd each other out."

Benjamin smiled. "That sounds like good advice. How did you know that?"

"I observed Grandma's herb garden. You can learn a lot by observing."

"What else have you learned by observing?"

"There are different ways to be smart. Some people are tool smart, some are farm smart, some are people smart and some are book smart."

"They are?"

"Of course, just look at our family. People can also have more than one way of being smart. Uncle Micah is tool and farm smart. Aunt Grace is people and book smart. Sadie is very tool smart – look how she paints those pretty pictures. She is not very people smart. I think it is because she cannot hear everything people say and that makes her shy. Libby is people and book smart just like Aunt Grace. Mama is people and tool smart because she is good at cooking and making things. You are book smart, but you are not farm and tool smart."

"That is very observant of you. I never thought about that before," Benjamin complimented his son. "What about your grandparents?"

"They are people, farm, tool and book smart. I think they are the smartest people I know."

"I agree. What about you?"

"I am farm and tool smart, but I am not book smart," he sadly shook his head. "I think that is why I disappoint you."

Benjamin swallowed hard. "I think you are very, very people smart too. The problem is I am so book smart that I am not people, tool or farm smart. I think we are opposites. In one way, that is a problem, because we do not often understand each other. In another way it is wonderful, because we can learn from one another."

Jacob smiled broadly, "Do you really think I could teach you something?"

"You already have taught me several things. Do you know when I was your age I was always getting into trouble with your grandfather? I would rather sit in my room and read a book than feed the stinky animals, or chop wood, or fetch water from the well. The worst thing in the world was weeding the garden!"

"No, the worst thing in the world is being stuck in school on a sunny day," Jacob contradicted. "It is not natural to sit indoors all day. How can I learn anything if I cannot move, or touch things, or observe how things work or grow? Did you really get in trouble all the time?"

"Yes I did. Having Micah being the perfect son only exacerbated the problem. I do not remember Micah ever getting in trouble, not even once."

"Maybe he did but you were too busy reading a book to notice," Jacob suggested.

Benjamin laughed out loud. "I would like to think so."

"Is that why you and Uncle Micah argue all the time?"

"We do not argue. We have serious, political discussions."

"Did you feel jealous of Uncle Micah?"

"No. I just feel inferior."

"I understand. That is how Abigail makes me feel."

"Please do not blame your sister for being book smart. I made you feel inferior not she. She and I are both book smart but not farm and tool smart. There is much you could teach both of us."

That afternoon Jacob and Benjamin did more than plant an herb garden; they sowed the seeds of a new relationship.

"Sir, there is a wagon of plants in front of the house," Joshua interrupted.

Benjamin looked up from his desk and through the front window. "Hannah! Abigail! They have arrived!" he called excitedly as he ran out the front door followed by the others.

"They do not look like much," Abigail stated with disappointment.

"What are they, sir?" even Joshua, the farm boy, did not recognize the unfamiliar bushes.

"These are lilacs. They may not be impressive now. In four years we will have a hedgerow of the most fragrant, light purple flowers you have ever seen. Where is Jacob?"

Hannah hesitated, "I believe he is with Limbo for the afternoon."

"Well, we have some planting to do today. I shall go get him," Benjamin sprinted in the direction of the Oxford House.

"Good day, Aunt Nabby. Have you seen my son?"

"Your Jacob is with Limbo, Benjamin"

As he quietly walked through the kitchen and headed toward Limbo's small room at the back of the house he could clearly hear his son's voice.

"When in the course of human events it becomes nek-nek"

"Necessary," Limbo corrected. The letter c usually sounds like a k. Sometimes it sounds like an s when it is followed by e or i."

"That makes no sense," Jacob grumbled.

"Well, it is true. Your father told me so."

"My father told you so?"

"Of course. Your father was the one who taught me to read and write. In fact he was not much older than you are when he started. Now it is only fair that I help you."

"Did you not learn to read when you were in school?"

"Jacob, men like me do not go to school. I cannot wait to see the expression on your father's face when you read this to him."

"Jacob?" Benjamin called loudly. "The lilacs have arrived."

"I have to go, Limbo."

"Syringa vulgaris is the Latin word for the common lilac. In Arabic it is laylak and in Persian it is nylac. They both mean blue.[1] Although these flowers will be purple," Benjamin explained as the two of them were placing the plants evenly spaced across the front yard. "Decades from now, these bushes will be taller than I am, providing privacy and protection from dirt and dust entering our open windows in the summer."

"Where did they come from?"

"Lilacs can be found from south eastern Europe to eastern Asia.[2] Thomas Jefferson planted lilacs at his home in Monticello before the war." [3]

"We got these from President Jefferson?"

"No," Benjamin laughed. "We got these from Portsmouth, New Hampshire."

The two of them worked silently for a half an hour before Jacob asked, "What did Mama mean when she said that you were my father and not my master?"

"What?"

"You know the day I spilt the ink and Mama came running in and said – "

"I remember. When your mother lived in Virginia she often saw slave owners hit their slaves."

"I did not know she lived in Virginia. I thought she came from Philadelphia."

"When she was a little girl she lived in Virginia until her father died in the war and then she went to live with relatives in Philadelphia. That is where I met her."

"She never tells us stories about when she was a little girl, like you tell us stories."

"I do not believe she had a happy childhood. Please do not ask her about it for I do not wish to upset her. Are we going to dig or are we going to talk all day?"

Eating his meals with the Millers was always fascinating to Joshua, for he never knew what topic the family would discuss next. Friday evening's supper was no exception.

"Papa, I wish to attend Fryeburg Academy," Abigail stated gravely.

"Abigail, eight-year-olds do not attend the Academy," Benjamin stated evading the issue.

"I mean when I am fourteen-years old I wish to attend Fryeburg Academy. It is not fair that girls are not allowed to attend when I am smarter than most of the boys at school."

"Have you been speaking with your cousin, Libby again?"

"No, sir. I have been speaking with Mama."

"Hannah?" Benjamin raised one eye brow at his smiling wife.

"Benjamin, I have two children and I want both of them to have the opportunities I never had. You are the first to admit that she is much advanced in her studies."

"She can take my place!" Jacob offered.

"You are very generous, son. However the rule is the academy is only for young men."

"Even if they are stupid?" Abigail argued.

Joshua stifled his laugh. "Perhaps, Abigail, you need to hire an attorney and go to court."

"Or my husband who serves as a trustee to the Academy can change the rule," Hannah smiled sweetly at Benjamin.

At that moment, Joshua knew that someday little Abigail would indeed attend Fryeburg Academy.

James and Sarah had graciously invited Joshua to Sunday dinners at the farm after church services. Joshua entered their foyer and looked at several paintings adorning the walls of the hall.

"Mr. Pierce, may I introduce you to my niece, Sadie," Benjamin smiled at the shy sixteen-year-old standing before them.

"Is this the talented, young lady who painted all the beautiful landscapes back at your house? It is my pleasure to finally meet you," Joshua smiled.

Sadie blushed and returned his smile.

"Are your paintings for sale? I would love to purchase one for my parents."

"Yes, sir. I have sold several here in town. Also my Uncle Ethan has sold several at his dress shop in Virginia."

"Your Uncle Ethan is a dress maker?"

Sadie burst out laughing. "No! Uncle Ethan is a cabinet maker, but my Aunt Olivia is the dress maker."

"Mr. Pierce, this is Sadie's sister, Libby."

"Elizabeth," Libby corrected her uncle.

Joshua tried not to stare at the beautiful eighteen-year-old woman. "It is a pleasure."

"Of course you know Alden," Hannah smiled at her nephew.

"So this is the young lad running in and out of your back door? Hello, Alden."

They entered the dining room where James and Micah were seated discussing tilling an additional two acres this summer. "Mr. Pierce, may I present my father, James Miller."

"It is indeed an honor, sir. Thank you for your kind invitation."

"You should thank my wife and Grace, for they did all the cooking," he laughed.

"You sir, must be Micah," Joshua shook his hand as Sarah and Grace entered carrying platters of cold meats and a crock of baked beans.

"May, I help you, Mrs. Miller?" Joshua offered as he took a platter from Sarah. "Back home I always brought the food to the table and helped to clear the table afterwards."

"Your mother taught you well," Sarah smiled with approval.

"I fear I had no sisters and was the youngest of seven boys," he replied.

Turning to Grace, "Mrs. Miller, I see where your daughters get their beauty."

Grace laughed, "Mr. Pierce, you may join us for dinner anytime!"

It was the best summer Jacob ever had. He rose at daybreak, completed his chores, weeded and watered his garden, ate breakfast with his family before heading off to Riverview Farm. He spent the mornings working with Alden, Uncle Micah and his grandfather before dinner. After his grandfather tutored him in reading for an hour, he returned to work on the farm for the rest of the afternoon. Every evening he ate supper, with his family and Mr. Pierce who by now felt like a member of the family.

Evenings were the best because that was when he had his father's undivided attention. Sometimes they practiced penmanship or reading; other times Benjamin read portions of *Pilgrim's Progress* which captured Jacob's imagination. The best evenings were when the two of them sat on the back steps watching the fireflies while Benjamin told him stories. Jacob learned how he was a descendant of William Bradford, one of the Pilgrims. He learned that he was named after his grandmother's brother, Jacob Bradford who fought at the battle of Lexington.

Sometimes his father read letters written to his grandmother by Abigail Adams. Through them he learned about the Continental Congress, the Boston Massacre, and the Boston Tea Party. His father told him stories of Aunt Grace was a little girl, living in a big house in Boston and the day when British soldiers moved into their home. He talked about the Constitutional Convention in Philadelphia back in 1787 and how he saw Benjamin Franklin, George Washington and James Madison enter and leave the hall every day. Little by little Jacob progressed through a well-worn copy of the New England Primer.

In a few short months, summer came to a close, the harvest was completed and Jacob returned to the village school. One November afternoon Jacob handed his father a note from his teacher.

November 1804

Dear Mr. Miller,

I am writing to tell you how pleased I am in Jacob's progress in school. Although his penmanship still leaves much to be desired, his reading and spelling has improved four fold...

Benjamin looked up at his son and smiled. "Jacob, I am so proud of you for your progress and perseverance."

Jacob's gaze fell to the ugly ink stain on his father's desk. "Sir, I never did apologize. I am truly sorry that I spilt the ink and ruined your desk."

"Jacob, that spilt ink was Providential. Do not feel sorry. I certainly do not."

XII

The Corps of Discovery

It was a cold, January evening when Benjamin and the family sat down by the hearth for their supper. Joshua wondered what political topic would be the focus for the evening's conversation. He was continually amazed at Benjamin's breadth of knowledge; he was equally impressed at the insights and opinions put forth by Hannah and the children. This was an extraordinary household.

After the blessing and while food was being passed Benjamin asked, "What can you tell me about the Louisiana Purchase?"

"I never heard of it," admitted Jacob as he buttered a slice of cornbread.

"Mr. Pierce?"

"I believe that President Jefferson purchased some land out west from France," Joshua offered.

"Indeed! Our esteemed Mr. Jefferson illegally purchased land from France for the grand sum of eleven million dollars and doubled the size of the country."

"I thought that would be a good thing," Jacob stated.

"Jacob, Papa is still angry that John Adams lost the election and blames Uncle Micah for voting for Jefferson," Abigail calmly explained.

Abigail never failed to amuse Joshua with her comments. "I do hope President Jefferson thanked your Uncle Ethan for his vote."

That comment made even Benjamin laugh. "Your point is well taken, sir. However we must consider both the pros and cons of the achievement. What are some of the advantages?"

"It doubled the size of the country and we did not even fight a war over it. That is a good thing," Jacob contributed. "There is now plenty of land for Americans to settle."

"New Orleans is the port of entry for the Mississippi River. Now that we own it and all that land we can freely navigate and trade on the river. This is invaluable as settlers continue to migrate west." Joshua failed to see any disadvantages to the purchase.

"True enough, Mr. Pierce. However, I ask you, is this sordid affair constitutional? With all of his talk of states' rights, Jefferson then turns around and usurps those rights by assuming the federal government has the authority to conduct this purchase. I doubt this treaty is legal. Napoleon Bonaparte could not constitutionally alienate it without the consent of the French Chamber.[1]

My concern is slavery. Slavery already existed in this territory under both the Spanish and the French. When Napoleon took possession of New Orleans from the Spanish in 1801, he sent a military force to secure it. Southerners feared if Napoleon freed the slaves in Louisiana, it might trigger slave uprisings elsewhere." [2]

"Do you mean like the slave revolt in Haiti?" Abigail asked.

"That is exactly what I mean."

"That would be a good thing, right?" Jacob asked.

"However, President Jefferson supported Congress in passing a law legalizing slavery in the territory."

"With a stroke of a pen President Jefferson expanded slavery to vast areas of the country," Hannah said softly. "What happens when these territories seek admission as states into the Union?"

"I fear they will be admitted as slave states."[3]

"If Napoleon just got it from Spain, why would he turn around and sell it?" Abigail asked.

"Napoleon does not need the land, but he does need the money. I do not trust that man, for he is both deceitful and ambitious. He is a tyrant."

"The French had a revolution and killed the king so they could be free," Abigail pointed out.

"I fear after all that bloodshed, all they did was trade one tyrant for another."

"Papa, what is in this territory? There could be silver and gold and new kinds of animals and monsters!" Jacob grew excited. "We should go exploring."

"That is exactly what Jefferson said when he sent Meriwether Lewis and William Clark and the Corps of Discovery on an expedition up the Mississippi River in canoes to explore.[4]

This brings me to my next topic," Benjamin smiled at his son. "Some time ago, your Aunt Grace found this in one of her father's old trunks. It is very old – written in French by one of their old Sea Captains who spent a winter among the Indians of Eastern Canada. These are sketches of some Passamaquoddy Indian canoes and instructions on how to build a birch bark canoe. This winter, you and I shall endeavor to make this canoe in Uncle Ethan's old workshop."

"You are going to build something?" Jacob asked in innocent disbelief. "With tools?"

"That is why you have to help me. By the summer, we will go exploring."

Hannah smiled with appreciation at her husband.

"You and I are going down the Mississippi?" Jacob excitedly asked.

Benjamin shook his head, "No. We are going to explore the Saco. I have crossed it a few times on the ferry, but I never explored it. We will study the plants and animals in our travels. We will be our own Corps of Discovery.

Saturday morning father and son dressed warmly with extra pairs of wool socks, fur-lined moccasins which laced up to their shins, fur mittens and hats and their great coats tightly buttoned. They hitched James' two horses, Samson and Delilah, to the wagon which held tools and two pairs of snowshoes and headed toward North Fryeburg.

"Father, look at all of these trees right here. Why are we driving to North Fryeburg to chop down trees?"

"There is a stand of cedar trees that we will look at. Because cedars are strong, light weight, flexible, and very easy to carve, the Indians knew they were the ideal trees to make canoes."

"I thought birch bark canoes were made of birch trees."

"According to the French log, cedar is the best material to build the frame. The frame will then be enveloped by birch bark. The bark is connected to the cedar with thin strips of spruce roots. We need to take this one step at a time."

With tools in hand, the two snow-shoed up a steep incline. "This tree looks good," Benjamin declared.

"Father, this tree looks dead," Jacob looked up at the forty-foot tree.

"A live tree would take months before it is seasoned and it would be months before we could even begin. Because this dead tree is already seasoned, we can begin right away. It will also be much lighter for us to carry back down to the wagon."

Jacob looked at his father in admiration. Benjamin smiled, "I spent many hours with your Uncle Ethan in the woods when I was a boy.

It took over one hour for Benjamin to chop down the young, dead tree. An eager Jacob quickly chopped off the branches.

"Who invented slavery?" Jacob asked his father.

"Satan did," Benjamin answered.

Jacob's eyes widened as he put down his hatchet. "He did?"

"Satan is the author of all evil. I cannot think of any evil greater than one man owning another like a piece of disposable property. We are all created in the image of God. How can one man even think to own someone created in His very image. Slavery is as old as civilization itself. Every civilization has practiced slavery; the Sumerians, the Egyptians, the Assyrians, the Babylonians, the Persians, the Greeks, the Romans, the Huns and the

Visigoths, the Ottomans, even the Hebrews. The feudal system of the Middle Ages had their poor serfs. Russia has serfs who are no better than slaves."

"Not all slaves are African?"

"No and not all Africans are slaves."

"I never knew that." With his curiosity now satisfied he changed the subject, "Papa, How big will our canoe be?"

"The sketches were for a canoe two and a half fathoms in length."

"What is a fathom?"

"A fathom is a unit of linear measure, approximately equivalent to six feet," Benjamin explained. "It is supposed to represent the distance between a man's two outstretched arms.'

"Then our canoe will be fifteen feet long. I like this kind of mathematics."

"Oh, no! I forgot to bring your grandfather's measuring tape."

"We do not need one. The axe handle is three feet long or a half of a fathom. Five axe handles will measure fifteen feet or two and a half fathoms."

"I never knew that," Benjamin smiled. "If you measure, than I will chop."

With a draw shave, the two of them took turns peeling the remaining bark. It was late afternoon when they carried the tree down the hill, and loaded the wagon. It was almost sunset when they returned the horses and the wagon to the barn.

Micah greeted them with a smile. "I underestimated you, Benjamin. I did not think you could chop down a tree by yourself."

"I had help," he admitted. Jacob could not remember ever feeling so proud.

Father and son returned home cold, exhausted, hungry and very pleased with themselves.

The next Saturday Micah, Alden and James were in the barn awaiting Benjamin and Jacob's arrival. "I have built many things in my life, but never a canoe. Would you mind if I lent a hand?" James offered.

"We are done with our chores. Alden and I could help for the morning," Micah volunteered.

"Today's work is pretty straight forward. We are going to split the log in half the long way and then in quarters and so forth." With wedges and froes the men began splitting the wood as they talked about Ethan's life in Virginia, Sadie's newest painting and Micah's proposal to sell milk, butter and cheese to the Oxford House. They discussed everything except politics.

By mid-morning James excused himself stating he needed to go back to the house to rest his old bones. Benjamin accompanied him and helped his father get comfortable in his favorite chair. Two hours later, Jacob found the two men sipping tea and discussing the Bill of Rights.

"Uncle Micah is almost done."

Benjamin turned to his son, tapped his right temple with his forefinger and smiled. "Smarter. Much smarter." Jacob laughed out loud.

On the fourth Saturday father and son left after breakfast and walked down River Street to the farm. "Why do people have slaves?" Jacob asked.

"I guess greed is the reason. As long as it is economically advantageous, most people will ignore the moral imperative."

"Are all slave owners bad?"

"Not all of them. Mr. Osgood's father, Samuel, bought Limbo from another man who mistreated him.[5] In Philadelphia, I knew many Quakers who bought slaves and treated them like members of their family. Some bought them for the sole purpose of giving them their freedom."

"Is that why you bought Mama?"

The blood drained from Benjamin's face as he looked at his son in disbelief. How could he possibly have known?

"I am truly sorry, Papa. I knew it was wrong to read those papers in your desk. But I saw your name and Mama's name and the word slave and I was curious."

"Who have you told?" Benjamin demanded.

"No one! I promise I never told anyone – not even Alden," he started crying. "I will never, ever tell anyone - I promise."

"Do not ever mention this to your mother. Do you understand?"

"I give you my word. I will never tell anyone."

"A man is only as good as his word," he reminded his son. "Make me a promise. If I should die before your mother does, I want you to place those papers in her coffin and bury them with her."

"Yes, sir. But Mama does not look like Limbo. She does not look like a slave. Why did you buy her?"

"Because I loved her and signed the papers giving her freedom. She loved me also and accepted my marriage proposal."

"Do you mean that I could have been a slave, too?"

"Under other circumstances you and your sister could have been born slaves."

Jacob looked up at his father. "I am proud to have you as my father."

"I am proud to have you as my son. However, we will never build that canoe if we stand in the road and talk all day."

By the beginning of May the fifteen foot long gunwales, all the ribs and sheathing were carved. Now it was time to search for the perfect white birch tree. "I know where we can find some promising birch trees," Benjamin said as he and Jacob started towards the woods.

"You do?" Jacob asked in surprise.

"Your Uncle Ethan would drag me out here to help him get birch bark strips for baskets."

After an hour's hike, they found a stand of birch trees.

"What about this one? Is this big enough?" Jacob pointed to a forty foot tree, eighteen inches across and a good twenty feet before the first branch. Father and son took turns chopping at the tree. Thirty minutes later their efforts were rewarded when the tree came crashing down - in the opposite direction that Benjamin intended.

"Your Uncle Micah will never hear about this," Benjamin warned with a grin.

"Hear about what?" Jacob laughed.

After marking off two and a half fathoms, Benjamin cut a deep, straight line with a sharp knife. To their surprise the bark began to spring off the trunk. "I remember Ethan telling me you had to wait until the sap stopped running for the bark to come off easily. I guess he knew what he was talking about." Triumphantly, father and son hiked back to the farm with the rolled up birch bark.

Benjamin and Jacob were in the barn showing Micah and Alden their prize when they heard a galloping horse stop in front of the farm house. They saw Simon Frye run into the house, run back onto his horse and gallop away. Libby came running into the barn with tears streaming down her face.

"Libby, what is wrong?" Micah asked as he ran up to his daughter.

"Reverend Fessenden has died!" she blurted.

Benjamin leaned back against the wall and swallowed hard. How he depended on the good pastor's prayers and sympathy when his sister died a quarter of a century ago! As a boy how he eagerly read all the books this kind scholar had lent him. Reverend Fessenden's letters from Fryeburg were an antidote to Benjamin's loneliness while he was at Harvard and in Philadelphia. It was the personal recommendation of this mentor that led to Benjamin's preceptorship of Fryeburg Academy. Benjamin would have surely fainted at his own wedding if his friend was not standing by encouraging him.

"Reverend Fessenden is the only pastor I ever had," lamented Alden.

"He is the only pastor that I remember," Micah agreed.

"Who will perform the funeral? Reverend Fessenden always spoke at everyone's funeral- even if he had to arrive on snowshoes!" Jacob asked in concern.

Benjamin spoke, "Your grandfather will. He was a minister of the Gospel in Cambridge before he became a farmer in Fryeburg. Jacob, we need to go home and tell your mother and sister." There would be no more working on the canoe that 5th of May, 1805.

Benjamin and Jacob were back to work the next Saturday. It was now time to shape the ribs. After soaking in a large kettle of steaming water for ten minutes, each wet rib was now pliable enough to bend and dry into the appropriate shape.

"Hello, Jacob," eleven-year-old Katie Wiley stood at the entrance of the barn and smiled. "My grandfather is visiting your grandfather. He said I could come and visit too."

"K-K-Katie," Jacob stammered. "Alden is not here. I think he is in the house."

"I did not come to see Alden. I came to see your canoe."

"Jacob, do you intend to introduce us?" Benjamin prodded his son.

"Katie, this is my father, Benjamin Miller. Father, this is Katie Wiley. She is the smartest girl in the whole school!"

She seemed pleased with the introduction. "How do you intend to put on the birch bark?

"We will split spruce roots and sew it on just like the Indians did."

"If I help you with the sewing, may I have a ride in the canoe?"

"Son, I believe that is a fair offer! We will not be sewing with needle and thread, however. We will first punch holes with an awl and then sew by pushing the spruce roots through the holes. Finally we will seal the seams with spruce pitch. Your help will be most appreciated.

Besides, according to the old log, the Passamaquoddy women did the bark sewing"

That week, Jacob recruited the assistance of the women in the family in exchange for rides in the canoe. He was pleasantly surprised that even his grandmother volunteered. "James, I think paddling down the Saco will be a delightful diversion."

After failing to find a good supply of black spruce within the vicinity, they settled upon using the roots of the plentiful white pine. "Are you sure white pine roots will work?" Jacob questioned.

"Uncle Ethan often used white pine roots in weaving his baskets. We will find out soon enough."

They found a stand of white pines with little undergrowth where the roots were near the surface. After prodding the ground with a hatchet, they discovered a root as thick as Benjamin's thumb. One chop with a hatchet severed it. They pulled up a six foot clear section of root before it subdivided. They continued until they had several dozen sections of pine root varying in length between four and eight feet.

Back at the barn they scraped off the scaly root bark. They were thrilled when the first root easily split in half after notching one end with a knife. However, it took two weeks of tedious, careful evening work to scrape and split their entire supply of roots.

The first Saturday in June, Benjamin set up the large maple syrup kettle in the side yard. Jacob and Alden made numerous trips to the well to fill the kettle with water as Benjamin kindled the fire beneath.

The day before, Jacob and Alden located a perfectly level section of the yard and designated it as the building bed. They made three dozen stakes two feet long from cedar scraps and drove them into the ground using the assembled gunwales with their thwarts as an outline.

Now they pulled up the stakes and the gunwale assembly leaving the holes behind. They rolled out the bark over the holes, replaced the gunwale assembly into position on top of the bark and weighed it down with several rocks.

Pouring hot water over the bark, they carefully and slowly bent the edges of the bark vertically up around the gunwales until they could replace the stakes. Working from the widest portion of the canoe, they forced the bark to snug up to the stakes by fastening short pieces of wood to the tops of the stakes, sandwiching the bark between them. As they approached the narrowing sides of the canoe, they needed to keep the bark even by cutting from the top down approximately every foot to prevent buckling.

When they completed this phase, the sheet of bark rested on the building bed in the basic shape of a canoe. After removing the rocks, they lifted the gunwale assembly, and replaced the rocks. James and Alden helped Benjamin and Jacob place and secure the gunwales in their final position. The four of them carefully folded the birch bark over the gunwales and trimmed away the excess.

"First thing Monday morning, Jacob and Alden can begin to punch holes with the awl in the birch bark directly under the gunwale."

Jacob thought it was a sin to waste a perfectly sunny Sunday afternoon sitting at home when he could be at work on the canoe. The first thing Monday morning, after a hasty breakfast, Jacob ran to the farm. He smiled when he found his eager grandfather starting the fire under the kettle so they could soak the roots. Jacob and Alden punched a series of three holes.

By nine o'clock Hannah and Abigail, Grace, Libby and Sadie appeared. "Is it time to sew?" Abigail asked.

"I believe this will be more like weaving a basket, than sewing," Grace explained for she had vast experience in basket making. The ladies took the wet roots and began to "sew" the canoe together. "We must keep our "stitches" straight, even and consistent."

Jacob was pleased when Katie arrived at eleven o'clock, "Am I too late?"

"Not at all dear," Grace smiled. I will demonstrate what you need to do."

Most of the "sewing" was done by supper. After work, Benjamin and Joshua arrived to shape the ends by inserting stem pieces. With the outside finished, they would begin completing the inside the next day.

Tuesday, Jacob found his grandfather heating up the kettle of water and Alden pouring buckets of hot water inside the canoe to soften the bark. When the bark appeared softened, the boys tipped the canoe over to drain the water. They placed the sheathing inside in an over lapping fashion and held them into place with the preformed ribs.

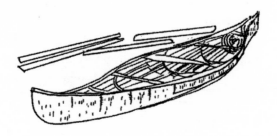

It was late June when father and son took the canoe on its maiden voyage. James had surprised them earlier in the summer by carving two maple paddles. The entire family stood on the banks of the Saco River waving good bye as if they were making a two-year journey rather than a four mile trip to Swan's Falls. Jacob could hardly contain his excitement while Benjamin was grinning ear to ear.

"I guess we will discover if we did an adequate job in sealing the seams with pine pitch," Jacob said as he began paddling.

After they rounded the first bend, they stopped so they could admire the view. "I think I will take Sadie for a ride. I bet she would love to paint this."

"Is that an eagle over head?" Benjamin pointed.

"Yes. Its nest is up that tree."

"What kind of trees are those?" Benjamin asked further downstream.

"If Uncle Ethan was here, he would know. We will take a closer look. Perhaps if we take a few leaves Grandpa could identify it."

Benjamin jumped out of the canoe first and tied it up to the tree. "Look at all those blueberry bushes! You need to return with Alden with several baskets tomorrow." After a half an hour of exploring they returned to the canoe.

They discovered a large sand bar further down the river, where a small stream joined the Saco on the left. "This looks like a perfect spot for a swim," Benjamin suggested. The two pulled the canoe up, undressed and carefully folded their clothes and neatly placed them in the canoe. Benjamin was the first to run into the river. "The water is cold!" he gasped.

"What did you expect? You are swimming in melted snow."

Every spring the snow-melt from the White Mountains flowed into the Saco as it made its journey to the Atlantic Ocean. Jacob laughed as he gingerly waded in. "It is not that cold!"

Benjamin grabbed him by the waist and threw him in. "Is it cold now?" The two laughed and splashed. H e did not remember hearing his father laugh as much as he did that afternoon. It was all too soon when they arrived at Swan's Falls. "We will end our journey here. In the future we will portage here and put in after the falls."

They scrambled to the bank, pulled the canoe out of the river and tipped it over to drain. Mrs. Swan waved to them from her yard. "Hello, boys. Someone is waiting for you," she smiled pointing to James Miller sitting in his wagon which he had parked in the shade.

"Father, you need not have done that."

"Yes I do, if I want to take your mother for canoe ride tomorrow," he winked.

"Can I come too?" Jacob asked eagerly.

"Well, we will need a guide."

That summer Jacob spent almost as much time on the river as he did on dry land. He and Alden picked gallons of blueberries and brought them home to their mothers. The cousins took Sadie to the sandbar and helped her set up her easel and paints; she painted while they swam.

One afternoon, he and Katie Wiley portaged at the falls and then paddled to Fryeburg Harbor. Katie, who grew up in a house full of brothers, was not afraid to climb trees, follow deer tracks or collect Indian arrow heads. She did not care if her pigtails became undone; she was not shy about taking off her shoes and stockings, hiking up her skirts above her knees so she could wade in the river.

The town's folk would smile and wave at James and Sarah leisurely floating down the river. Some would call out to Jacob and Alden, "Hey look! There goes Lewis and Clark!" The boys would grin and wave. Jacob started a rock collection and went "mining for gold". Benjamin laughed and said he doubted that they would discover gold, but they might find some amethyst or tourmaline. Jacob took his mother and sister for rides. One day, even Mr. Pierce joined Jacob and Benjamin and went for a swim.

Sadly, at the end of October Jacob had to store the canoe for the winter in Uncle Micah's barn. "Jacob, do you think you could teach Alden and me to make a canoe this winter? We could have canoe races next summer," Micah smiled.

Jacob Freeman Miller was convinced he was the luckiest boy alive.

XIII

A Promise

"I did not take you to be a coward, Micah," Benjamin quietly challenged his brother.

"I did not take you to be a fool!" Micah exploded in an unusual display of anger.

"Benjamin, perhaps you should start at the very beginning," James calmly suggested as the three men sat in the drawing room with the door closed, the curtains drawn and two candles flickering on the mantle.

"Here is Ethan's letter," Benjamin handed it to his father to read aloud.

> *May 1, 1806*
> *Williamsburg, Virginia*
>
> *Dear Benjamin,*
> *I am shipping you one large, man's mahogany armoire via Philadelphia.*
> *Ethan*

"It means that Ethan is helping a large, male slave to escape to Philadelphia, where he will be sent to us, who will see him off to Canada. There are many abolitionists in Philadelphia who have spent years organizing a series of safe houses from Virginia to Canada."

"You put Ethan up to this," Micah accused. "He would never do something like this on his own."

"You are wrong. Ethan approached me in a letter two years ago. He already knew about the promise I made to the Quakers that I would someday use my home as a safe house, but I never asked him to become involved."

"That is the real reason you moved to Fryeburg, to keep your promise?" his brother asked.

"No, I moved up north to keep my promise. I moved to Fryeburg to be with my family."

"You moved to Fryeburg to endanger your family," Micah corrected. "We are not Quakers."

"Are we not Christians? Are we to do nothing in the face of evil?"

"It is against the law," Micah simply stated. "Are we to break the law? What would happen if everyone decided to break the law simply because they disagreed with it?"

"We are called to obey man's law unless obeying the law breaks God's law. We are called to obey the higher law."

"You are a lawyer. Are you not required to uphold the law?"

James interjected, "Benjamin, would your energies be best served in changing the law? The abolition of slavery would free all the slaves. Smuggling slaves to freedom could only save a few."

"Yes, I intend to work on changing the law. However, that could take years, perhaps several generations. I fear it will never happen in my lifetime."

"We are stealing another man's property," Micah argued. "We will be no better than horse thieves."

"Horses are not created in the image of God," he countered. "Father, you decide. Micah and I will abide by your decision."

"This is not my decision to make for it will affect all of us. Discuss this with your wives and children and pray for the Lord's wisdom. In two days all of us will meet to decide."

Two evenings later all eleven Millers congregated in the drawing room. James began, "You all know why we are here. I wish to listen to everyone's thoughts before we make any decisions."

Grace was the first to speak. "My family has made a handsome profit in the building and selling of slave ships. I think of those poor souls who lost their freedom because of those ships while I sipped tea in porcelain tea cups. It is only just that I now help those who are in misery."

Hannah smiled at Grace with admiration "My early childhood in Virginia was deeply affected by the sufferings I witnessed by the slaves. How would we feel if someone sold our children from us or…" Hannah could not continue. Jacob reached out and held his mother's hand.

"I could help. No one would ever expect a twelve-year-old in smuggling slaves," Jacob offered.

"Or two twelve-year-olds," Alden volunteered.

"They will need food for the journey. Libby and I can prepare supplies," Sadie looked directly at her father.

"It is cold in Canada, I can knit hats and mittens," Abigail continued.

"Abigail is right," Sarah agreed. "The first thing in the morning I will sit down at my loom and weave blankets."

James turned to his eldest son, "Micah?"

"I believe that my family has decided," he quietly replied.

It was now time for James to speak. "Micah, you made a valid point the other evening when you stated that as citizens we are not free to pick and choose which laws to obey and disobey. In this country we are free to elect our officials and to make new laws or change old ones.

I searched the Scriptures for answers. In the Book of Daniel four young Hebrews named Daniel, Shadrach, Meshach and Abednego were taken captive by the Babylonians. There they learned the language and the customs; they served a pagan king and obeyed their laws. However when King Nebuchadnezzar's laws opposed the law of the true God of Abraham, Isaac and Jacob, these godly men stood fast. Daniel chose to faithfully pray to only his God and face the lion's den rather to worship another. Shadrach, Meshach and Abednego refused to bow down and worship a golden statue and faced the fiery furnace.

At one time it was illegal for the common man to read the Scriptures in their native tongue for themselves. Where would we be today if men like William Tyndale, John Wycliffe or Jan Huss refused to break man's laws? I believe that Benjamin's assertion that we are called to obey man's law until it contradicts God's law is consistent with Scripture.

This has not been an easy decision for me to make. In light of verse 15 in the 24th chapter of the Book of Joshua,

I say 'As for me and my house, we shall serve the Lord'. May the Lord protect us."

June 4, 1806 was an extraordinary day. Most of the town attended the dedication of the new, two-storied Fryeburg Academy building at its new location in the center of the village. Benjamin Miller with the other trustees, the new preceptor, Reverend Amos Jones Cook and Reverend Nathaniel Porter all sat solemnly in the front facing the large audience. Many speeches were made that day; however, the Millers sat waiting for Benjamin's announcement.

"The trustees are of the opinion that it will be expedient to employ a Preceptress for the summer quarters to instruct young ladies in needlework, embroidery and painting, and likewise to assist in the instruction of reading, writing and English grammar.[1] It is my pleasure to introduce our Instructress of Females, Miss Isabella Child[2] and her assistant, Miss Elizabeth Miller."

Reverend Porter delivered the benediction. "I close this discourse with the short benediction that you and your children may enjoy and improve all offered advantages for instruction in the knowledge of God, and useful literature. That generations successively rising up in their fathers' stead, may be the exemplary patrons of truth, the firm friends of education and order, the props and ornaments of civil and religious society, till the sun shall rise and set no more." [3]

Most of the crowd was content to linger in the front yard of the Academy conversing with friends and neighbors. Benjamin stood talking with a circle of men.

"Papa," Jacob interrupted, "Can Alden and I go canoeing this afternoon?"

"It is a beautiful day for an excursion down the Saco," Benjamin agreed. "When all your chores at the farm are completed, you may go canoeing. In fact, we will load the canoe on the wagon and I will drive you to Center Conway to begin your journey. Mr. Pierce, will you kindly take my one o'clock appointment?"

The men smiled at Jacob's enthusiasm as he went running down the street yelling, "Alden! Alden, we can go! We can go!"

Sarah, Grace and Hannah were talking with the ladies when Sarah invited, "Hannah, please have the family join us for supper. It shall not be fancy, but we will celebrate this occasion."

Several young men, who were hoping to escort Libby home, were disappointed when Joshua Pierce easily fell into step with her and headed down the street. Abigail ran and soon caught up with them. "I told you I would go to Fryeburg Academy!" she beamed.

"Yes, you did," Joshua smiled down at the earnest ten-year old.

"When I grow up, I am going to be an attorney just like Papa."

"Abigail, you are a special young lady and I believe you will do whatever you please," he laughed.

"Libby, why did Papa call you Elizabeth?"

"Because that is my name. Libby is a child's name and I am no longer a child."

Abigail made a face, ran off after Sadie who was walking with her father and Mr. and Mrs. Weston.

No one paid particular attention as Benjamin drove the wagon with the boys and the canoe and slowly left Fryeburg for Conway. No one in Conway or Fryeburg paid much attention to the two boys talking and laughing as they paddled down the Saco.

Alden and Jacob waved as they passed Mr. Weston standing by the side of his house on the bank of the river. Mrs. Weston smiled as she watched the two excited boys across the street jump out of the canoe, pull it up the bank, and properly tip it over to ensure that any water left in it would drain.

"Good, we are not late for supper," Alden yelled. The two boys raced to the farm house as Benjamin, Hannah and Abigail entered the front yard.

Anyone passing by could have observed the eleven of them seated in the dining room, eating, and talking. Later, the men sat in the drawing room conversing while the ladies washed the dishes and cleaned up. Just before sunset, Benjamin, Hannah and Abigail headed home as Micah, Alden and Jacob entered the barn to do some chores.

It was well after ten o'clock when Mrs. Weston, who could not sleep, arose from her bed and looked out the bedroom window. There she saw Jacob and Limbo with his floppy, black felt hat and shock of white hair leave the Miller's large barn and walk slowly up the field heading towards Benjamin's house. She watched the two figures by the light of a half moon walk up to the back door where Hannah was there to greet them.

"Goodness, that child should have been in bed hours ago," she muttered before returning to her own bed.

"Come with me," Hannah spoke quietly as she took the African by the arm and led him to the basement stairs. "Thank you, Jacob, now take this candle and go directly to bed. Your job is done.

Here is a sack of supplies – food, candles, flint, some warm clothes and a blanket. Take this on your journey," Hannah instructed as she escorted the young man down the steps. "My husband will explain the rest." she whispered, nodding toward Benjamin, who was anxiously waiting for them in the basement holding a candle. She quickly went up the stairs and closed the cellar door before the African could reply.

"Here is your guide for the rest of the trip," Benjamin explained to 'Limbo', as the real Limbo stepped from the shadows. "Are you ready? Have you had some rest?"

"Yes, sir," he replied as he took off the hat and attempted to shake the white talcum powder from his black hair. "I slept while I was hiding under the canoe. Please thank the boys for my first canoe ride."

"May I have my hat back?" Limbo asked. "A friend gave it to me many years ago. My head does not feel right without it," he explained as he picked up his own sack of supplies and slung it over his shoulder.

Benjamin slowly pushed open a false wall that led to a small, secret room which Ethan had painstakingly designed and built years ago. "Well, Limbo, this is it," Benjamin could feel the lump rising in his throat. "You have been my most loyal friend." He was thankful that the shadows were hiding the tears streaming down his face. "Remember, Limbo, 'And the Lord, He it is that doth go before thee; he will be with thee, he will not fail thee, neither forsake thee: fear not neither be dismayed'", he quoted Deuteronomy 31:8.

The two men headed toward the secret, granite-lined tunnel.[4] "Mr. Benjamin?" Limbo turned around. "What about the Osgoods?"

"Do not worry, Limbo, for they will be handsomely compensated for the loss of your services. I will discreetly handle the legalities."

"Mr. Benjamin, I do not know how to thank you – for this, for teaching me, for treating me like a friend."

"You are a friend. You are my best friend. Micah and Ethan are my brothers, but you are my friend. Let me pray before you leave. God in Heaven, I entrust to You the care of these two good men. Protect them, care for them and lead them both to freedom. Amen."

"Mr. Benjamin?"

"Benjamin, Limbo. My name is just Benjamin. My family and friends simply call me Benjamin."

"Good bye, Benjamin."

"Good bye, Limbo." He watched the two men disappear into the darkness of the tunnel. He slipped out of the secret room, quietly replaced the false wall, quickly went up the basement steps and closed the door. "Good bye, Limbo, my friend." he whispered.

The next morning the family ate their breakfast in silence; it was understood they were never to speak about the events of last night. "Benjamin, am I late for breakfast?" Limbo popped his head into the kitchen smiling ear to ear. There was silence and many blank stares from all others at the table. "That poor soul was scared half to death. I could hardly understand what he was saying. He has a mother and three little sisters left behind. I was thinking if I go all the way to Canada, I would have freed one slave."

"Two," Hannah corrected.

"Right, two slaves, counting me. But if I came back I could help free dozens of slaves."

"But, Limbo, what about your own freedom?" Benjamin asked in disbelief.

"Thirty years ago, your father told me that there are only two kinds of men – those who are slaves to sin and those who are free in Christ. My freedom is in Christ."

"Yes, of course. But, Limbo, what about your freedom in this life?"

"Benjamin, I am free. I freely chose to help one man escape, and I freely returned. And I freely choose to help others find freedom. I am still free to decide if and when I want to go to Canada or if I want to return each time. I am free, Benjamin. I am free."

The Judah Dana House

J udah Dana, the first attorney in Fryeburg, built a large colonial house in the village at the corner of River Street and Main Street in 1816. John Stuart Barrows writes of the many accomplishments of Mr. Dana in his book *Fryeburg An Historical Sketch*.

An article entitled "A Tunnel under Main Street" in the Fryeburg Historical Newsletter, Volume II, No. 4, October, 1993 provides some history on the tunnel under Main Street from the Judah Dana House to the former Eckley Stearns residence across the street. No one knows the approximate date the tunnel was constructed. According to a study by Ben Conant, the Underground Railroad started in Maine in 1830 and went through Fryeburg to Sweden, Maine.

In a 1993 interview, Fryeburg physician Dr. Kenneth Dore stated, "The tunnel under the road is common knowledge. That was an escape route for slaves and there was another route after that, like Fryeburg Harbor, which was one of the places where the slaves went."

Dr. Dore's daughter, Emily Dore Fletcher, librarian of the Fryeburg Library, recalls exploring the entrance to the tunnel in 1956 when the house was being torn down to build the Fryeburg Post Office. Bob Hatch and his grade school friends explored the tunnel – usually after the demolition crew left for the day. The walls and ceiling were granite with the ceiling about five feet high and the width such that a youth could easily touch both sides. The floor appeared to be firm earth with perhaps stone under it.

I am a story teller, not a historian. Judah Dana is one of the inspirations for the fictional adult character, Benjamin Miller. The Judah Dana House, pictured above is my inspiration for Benjamin's house. The story of "A Tunnel under Main Street" is my inspiration for *A Secret and A Promise*.

Fryeburg Academy

F ryeburg Academy is an independent, secondary school that serves a widely diverse population of local day students and boarding students across the nation and around the world. Maintaining a lasting tradition of democracy and academic excellence since 1792, Fryeburg Academy is one of the oldest schools in the country and in Maine (then part of Massachusetts). It was also one of the first secondary schools to accept women and African Americans.

Today, Fryeburg Academy serves 657 students drawing from our nine local communities as well as from around the world – including China, Korea, Vietnam, Germany, Spain, Thailand, Turkey, Russia, Denmark, and Sweden as well as from many US States. Nearly all graduates of the Academy move on to some form of post-secondary education.

Timothy Scott
Director of Development
Fryeburg Academy

Discussion Questions

1. Discuss the cultural, economic and political importance of Philadelphia from 1787 – 1800.
2. Why did the nation's capital move to Washington, D.C.?
3. What were the plights of Loyalists during and after the American Revolution?
4. Why were Alexander Hamilton's money reforms in 1792 necessary? Compare and contrast the monetary system of 1792 to ours today. Which one do you prefer?
5. What was Shay's Rebellion? What were Samuel Adam's and Thomas Jefferson reactions to it? Would you have been for or against it?
6. Describe the mission, the student body, the curriculum and the rules and regulations of Fryeburg Academy in 1792. How does it compare to your local high school today?
7. Define the concept of "inalienable rights". Where did this term originate? List some of the political thinkers in the past that may have influenced the writers of the Declaration of Independence.

8. Benjamin states that "ideas have consequences. What you believe will determine how you will act." Do you agree or disagree with that statement? Support your answer.

9. How did Benjamin's belief that slaves have inalienable rights affect his decisions?

10. Do you believe that American citizens have the right to break the law? If yes, what laws do you believe should be broken? What criteria should be used when making that decision? What options do American citizens have when facing a law they disagree with?

11. What is freedom?

12. Does slavery exist today? If so, where?

End Notes

Chapter I The Homecoming

1. Handout reprinted from Mercer Museum Collection – Tools and Trades of America p. 117- 118.

    Description of opened, antique tool box as seen at the Farm Museum at the Fryeburg Fair in Fryeburg, ME in October 2011

    Description of a work bench as seen at the Cabinet Maker's Shop in Colonial Williamsburg in Williamsburg, VA
2. Description of furniture as seen at the Cabinet Maker's Shop in Colonial Williamsburg in Williamsburg, VA.
3. http://en.wikipedia.org/wiki/FranklinStove.

Chapter II Philadelphia

1. John S. Barrows, <u>Fryeburg Maine An Historical Sketch</u> (Fryeburg, ME: Pequawket Press, 1938) pg. 242
2. David McCullough, <u>John Adams</u> (New York: Simon & Schuster, 2001) pg. 81.

3. Daniel J. Boorstin, <u>The Americans The Colonial Experience</u> (New York: Vintage Books, 1958) pg. 308

4. Catherine Drinker Bowen, <u>Miracle at Philadelphia</u> (Boston: Little, Brown and Company, 1966) pg. 3

5. Ibid.

6. Ibid.

7. http://www.calliope.org/shay2.html

8. Ibid.

9. http://wwwushistory.org/us15a.asp

10. http://www.calliope.org/shay2.html

11. Ibid.

12. Ibid.

13. http://www.calliope.org/shay2.html

14. Bowen, pg.

15. McCullough, pg.

16. Henry F. Graff, Editor, <u>The Presidents a Reference History</u> (New York: Simon & Schuster McMillan, 1996) pg. 40

17. David McCullough, pg. 78-80

18. Daniel Boorstin, pg. 310

19. Daniel Boorstin, pg. 308

20. Ibid.

21. David McCullough, pg. 78-80

22. http://en.wikipedia.org/wiki History_of_ Washington_D.C.

23. Ibid.

24. Ibid.

25. John S. Barrows, pg. 125.

26. Paul Johnson, <u>The History of the American People</u> (New York: HarperCollins, 1997) pg. 171

27. Daniel Boorstin, pg. 61
28. Ibid.
29. As seen at the Milliner's Shop in Colonial Williamsburg, Williamsburg, VA in August 2011
30. As seen at the Cabinet Maker's Shop in Colonial Williamsburg, VA in August 2011
31. Conversations with staff at Colonial Williamsburg, August 2011.
32. http://en.wikipedia.org/wiki/Marco_Polo

Chapter III A Secret

1. Now called Pine Hill, Portland Press, June 8, 1892
2. John S. Barrows, pg. 126

Chapter IV The Harvest

1. Debra Friedman and Jack Larkin, Editors. <u>Old Sturbridge Village Cook</u> (Guilford, CT: Three Forks, 1984) pg. 101
2. Friedman and Larkin, pg. 184
3. Friedman and Larkin, pg. 156
4. Friedman and 4Larkin pg. 152
5. http://www.alcasoft.com/soapfact/historycontent.html

Chapter V The Preceptor

1. Handout from a 2001 workshop at the Remick Country Doctor Museum and Farm in Tamworth, N.H.
2. John S. Barrows, Class of 1884, "Historical Sketch of Fryeburg Academy" written in 1892
3. Bobbie Kalman, 18<u>th</u> Century Clothing (New York: Crabtree Publishing Company, 1993) pg.20
4. John S. Barrows, "Historical Sketch of Fryeburg Academy"
5. John S. Barrows, <u>Fryeburg Maine An Historical Sketch</u> (Fryeburg, ME: Pequawket Press, 1938) pg. 118.
6. Gary Amos and Richard Gardiner, <u>Never Before in History</u> (Richardson, TX: Foundation for Thought and Ethics, 2004) pg. 73
7. John S. Barrows, Historical Sketches of Fryeburg Academy.
8. Gary Amos, pg. 75.
9. Joegil K. Lundquist and Jeanne L. Lundquist, <u>English from the Roots Up</u> Medina, WA: Literacy Unlimited Publications, 2003) pg. 10.
10. Joegil and Jeanne Lundquist, pg. 22
11. http://en.wikipedia.org/wikicoinage_Act_of_1792
12. Ibid.
13. http://Answers.com_Coinage_Act_of_1792
14. Ibid.
15. http://en.wikipedia.org/wikicoinage_Act_of_1792
16. Gary Amos, pg. 16-17
17. Ibid
18. Gary Amos, pg. 5
19. Gary Amos, pg. 6-11

20. Gary Amos, pg. 13
21. Gary Amos, pg. 62
22. Gary Amos, pg. 63
23. Gary Amos, pg. 65
24. Gary Amos, pg. 71

Chapter VI Family

1. http://en.wikipedia.org/wiki/Fugitive_Slave_Act_of_1793

Chapter VII Hannah's Choice

1. "Tavern Night Recipes" (published by Remick Country Doctor Museum and Farm, Tamworth, NH, 9/25/10) pg. 7
2. Debra Friedman, pg. 162-163
3. Sodium bicarbonate used in cooking. Baking Soda. Origin 1830-1840 Americanism www.thefreedictionary.com
4. Debra Friedman, pg. 159

Chapter IX The Cabinet Maker

1. Barrows, pg. 85
2. Barrows, pg. 90
3. Natural Pigments Catalog of Professional Artists' Materials. (Willitis, CA, 2009) pg.11.

4. Artie Wallert, Editor, <u>Still Lifes: Techniques and Style</u> (Zwollie, Netherlands: Waanders Publishing, 2000) pg. 11
5. Interview with artist Jon Marshall in his studio in Denmark, Maine of 4/25/12.
6. <u>Natural Pigments</u> Catalog, pg. 5
7. Artie Wallert, pg. 7-9
8. Ibid.
9. Bruce Robertson, <u>Marguerite Makes a Book</u> (Los Angeles: J. Paul Getty Museum, 1999) fold-out pages
10. Pen and ink sketch by E. Barbour, 1976
11. Marriage Records in the Fryeburg Historical Society Archives

Chapter XI Split Ink

1. http://arboretum.harvard.edu/plants/features
2. http://en.wikipedia.org/wiki/Syringa_vulgaris
3. http://arboretum.harvard.edu/plants/features

Chapter XII The Corps of Discovery

1. http://en.wikipedia.org/wiki/Louisiana_Purchase
2. ibid
3. ibid
4. ibid
5. John S. Barrows, pg. 241-243

XIII A Promise

1. Barrows, pg.130
2. Barrows, pg. 131
3. Barrows, 127
4. "A Tunnel under Main Street", Fryeburg Historical Newsletter Volume II. No.4, 1993

Bibliography

Books:

Adney, Edwin Tappan and Chapelle, Howard I. The Bark Canoes and Skin Boats of North America. Washington, D.C. Smithsonian Institution. Bulletin no. 230, 1964.

Amos, Gary and Gardiner, Richard. Never Before in History .Richardson, TX. Foundation for thought and Ethics. 2004.

Barrows, John Stuart. Fryeburg, Maine an Historical Sketch. Fryeburg, ME. Pequawket Press. 1938.

Boorstin, Daniel J. The Americans: The Colonial Experience. New York. Vintage Books. 1958.

Boorstin, Daniel J. Editor. We Americans. Washington, D.C. National Geographic Society. 1975.

Bowen, Catherine Drinker. Miracle at Philadelphia: The Story of the Constitutional Convention. Boston, MA. Little, Brown and Company. 1966.

Calkins, Carroll C., Editor. The Story of America. Pleasantville, NY. The Reader's Digest Association. 1975.

Gaynor, James M. and Hagedorn, Nancy L. <u>Tools Working Wood in Eighteenth-Century America.</u> Williamsburg, Virginia. The Colonial Williamsburg Foundation. 1993.

Johnson, Paul, <u>A History of the American People</u>. New York. Harper Collins. 1998.

McCullough, David. <u>John Adams. </u>New York. Simon & Schuster. 2001

Articles:

"A Tunnel under Main Street" <u>Fryeburg Historic Newsletter Volume II. No. 4,</u> 1993

"Centennial of One of Maine's Old Academies" Portland Press June 8, 1892

"Historical Sketch of Fryeburg Academy" J.S. Barrows Class of 1884

Scrapbook from Fryeburg Historical Society

Internet Websites:

http://en.wikipedia.org/wiki/FranklinStove.
http://www.ushistory.org/us15a.asp.
http://www.calliope.org/shay2.html.
http://en.wikipedia.org/wiki History_of_Washington _DC.
http://en.wikipedia.org/wiki/Marco_Polo.
http://www.alcasoft.com/soapfact/historycontent.html.
http://en.wikipedia.org/wikicoinage_Act_of_1792.
http://Answers.com_Coinage_Act_of_1792.
http://en.wikipedia.org/wiki/Fugitive_Slave_Act _of_1793.
http:/arboretum.edu/plants/features.html.

http://en.wikipedia.org/wiki/Syringa_Vulgaris.
http://en.wikipedia.org/wiki/Louisina_Purchase.

Illustrations:

1. Original drawing by Wayne O'Donal of Making a Cider Press
2. Drawing by Wayne O'Donal from www.alcasoft.com
3. Drawing by Wayne O'Donal based upon a 2001 handout from Remick Country Doctor Museum and Farm on "How to Make a Quill".
4. Drawing by Wayne O'Donal of Canoe Construction, from Adney and Chapelle, fig. 38, p. 45
5. Drawing by Wayne O'Donal of Canoe Construction, from Adney and Chapelle, fig. 45, p. 53
6. Drawing of the Judah Dana House from a 1976 pen and ink sketch by E. Barbour
7. Drawing of the original Fryeburg Academy of 1792, from an 1892 pen and ink sketch by John Stuart Barrows
8. The Fryeburg Academy Building built in 1806, duplicated from an 1892 pen and ink sketch by John Stuart Barrows

About the Author

June O'Donal is a nineteen-year homeschooling veteran who believes that history is fascinating and relevant; history textbooks are boring and irrelevant. History – the story of people and their ideas – is best learned from "living books"; biographies, autobiographies and historical fiction and non-fiction.

History must be taught in chronological order if we are to understand how the beliefs and actions of one generation impact future generations. It must include more than names and dates. We need to understand the technology, the literature, the culture, political and religious beliefs of each era.

June lives with her husband and two college-aged children in Maine.

About *The Fryeburg Chronicles*
www.thefryeburgchronicles.com

The Fryeburg Chronicles is a series of educational, family-friendly, historical novels set in the town of

Fryeburg, Maine. The fictional Miller family interacts with nonfictional historical figures.

Book I The Amazing Grace, published in 2011, explores some of the events in the founding of this rural New England town and events in Boston during the American Revolution. A spoiled, wealthy orphan from Boston named Grace Peabody comes to live with the Millers, a humble, farm family in Fryeburg who are mourning the death of their daughter/sister. Grace learns the skills to survive on a farm as she discovers the meaning of love and acceptance.

Book III Portraits of Change, planned for 2013, opens in the year 1819. The world is changing too fast for Micah Miller. After the funeral for James Miller, the family discovers slave catchers in their barn who are searching for a runaway slave. As Sarah is coping with widowhood, her grandchildren are struggling to find their place in the world. Much to Micah's chagrin, his children leave Riverview Farm to pursue adventures and opportunities.

One consequence of the Missouri Compromise is Maine becomes a state. The honorable Benjamin J. Miller leaves for Portland for three weeks to help write the Maine State Constitution and begins his career in politics. Hannah Miller is concerned that her intellectual daughter Abigail, preceptress of Fryeburg Academy is "passed her bloom" and will never marry. Jacob and Kate devote their lives to keeping Benjamin's promise and recruit like-minded town's folk to help.

After a ten-year absence and a personal tragedy, Mr. Joshua Pierce returns to Fryeburg with hopes of starting his life over.

The Fryeburg Chronicles are available wherever books and eBooks are sold. Produced and printed in the USA.

Visit us on Facebook to view photographs of a homemade cider press and birch bark canoe, and the cabinet maker's and dress maker's shop in Colonial Williamsburg. We are always posting new information and photos as I continue my research!

CPSIA information can be obtained at www.ICGtesting.com
Printed in the USA
BVOW070857100712

294759BV00001B/1/P